"I'm not that girl anymore, Tobias."

"Josie," he said, his eyes serious now, "whatever happened, whatever you're afraid of, I will handle it—for both of us."

Tears burned but Josie held tightly to her control. "It is my burden only, Tobias."

Before she knew what was happening, he sat down beside her. He took her hand in his, careful that no one would notice. "I made you something."

He slipped a warm piece of wood between their laced fingers. "I will carry your burdens, Josie."

Josie couldn't speak, couldn't move. The world around her seemed to recede as Tobias held her hand in his, the carving warm between them, the world away from them. The touch of his skin ricocheted through her system like a ray of warm sunshine, bringing a peace she hadn't felt in years. She lifted her hand and saw the delicate butterfly he'd shaped out of what looked like an exotic wood.

"Tobias," she whispered, ready to pour out her heart.

Tobias stood, his expression full of love and understanding. And hope...

With over seventy books published and millions in print, **Lenora Worth** writes award-winning romance and romantic suspense. Three of her books were finalists in the ACFW Carol Awards, and her Love Inspired Suspense novel *Body of Evidence* became a *New York Times* bestseller. Her novella in *Mistletoe Kisses* made her a *USA TODAY* bestselling author. Lenora goes on adventures with her retired husband, Don, and enjoys reading, baking and shopping…especially shoe shopping.

Visit the Author Profile page
at Harlequin.com for more titles.

Seeking Refuge

Lenora Worth

LOVE INSPIRED
INSPIRATIONAL ROMANCE

LOVE INSPIRED®
INSPIRATIONAL ROMANCE

ISBN-13: 978-1-335-42967-4

Seeking Refuge

Copyright © 2020 by Lenora H. Nazworth

This edition published by arrangement with Harlequin Books S.A.

For questions and comments about the quality of this book, please contact us
at CustomerService@Harlequin.com.

Love Inspired
22 Adelaide St. West, 40th Floor
Toronto, Ontario M5H 4E3, Canada
www.Harlequin.com

Printed in U.S.A.

Seek the Lord, and his strength:
seek his face evermore.
                    —*Psalm* 105:4

Dedicated to all the silent women out there
holding pain inside their hearts.

Chapter One

The house across the footbridge looked less sinister and sad in the spring.

Josie Fisher sat on the bench near the *grossmammi haus* and wished she could forget the other home that stood stark white, empty and waiting, off in the distance. She'd grown up in that house, and each time she went near it, the memories tore through her like a thunderstorm.

But today, with the spring wind in the air and flowers blooming all around, Josie felt hope in her heart. The early daffodils and dandelions her sister-in-law, Raesha, had planted around the yard lifted their determined heads to the sun. The old oaks and red maples were lush with new leaves. The herb garden behind the main house was coming along nicely. She could almost smell the fresh mint and basil, the dill and oregano. Josie watched as a robin pecked at the grass near the hat shop. She and Naomi had planted sunflowers there. It would take a while for those to grow and bloom.

Turning her head to the sun, Josie remembered Naomi Bawell's sage advice.

"Look at the sunflowers, Josie. See how they lift their faces toward the sky. They seek *Gott*'s love, same as we do."

Josie loved Naomi Bawell and clung to her as if she was indeed Josie's true grandmother. Naomi and Josie lived in the small *grossmammi haus* located behind the main house on the Bawell farm. Lived together and watched out for each other, as a *grossmammi* and *kinder* should. Josie felt safe there inside the solid walls with the tiny kitchen and living room, two bedrooms and a washroom in the back.

A breezeway separated their apartment from the rambling main house where her brother, Josiah, lived with his wife, Raesha, and their six-month-old son, Daniel.

And with little Dinah.

Josie's daughter by birth, but their daughter now to raise Amish. After they were married, they'd officially adopted Dinah.

Over two years ago, Josie had left three-month-old Dinah on the Bawell porch. Hard to believe that tiny baby girl was now walking and jabbering, her mischievous smile as bright as the sunshine.

You ran away and left your child. The voice that echoed inside her head made Josie look down at her dark blue tennis shoes.

But she is safe now and healthy and happy, and so are you. That voice made her look up again. Toward the sky.

"I did the right thing."

Yes, she'd done the right thing after being attacked by an *Englisch* boy. She'd felt it necessary to leave her baby with someone who could love her and take care of her. The Bawells had always been kind to Josie when she was little and afraid.

Now she was an adult but still so horribly afraid. She rarely left the property except to attend church and occasionally go to the general store. She'd been ruined by a man who'd later done the same thing to an *Englisch* girl, and because that girl also had a powerful family, Drew Benington had stood trial and had been sent to jail. After that, another girl had come forward to testify. Josie's friend Sarah had written to her about his arrest and the trial since they'd all known him. Sarah had no idea what had happened to Josie, but Josie's relief after reading her friend's letter had been short-lived. What if Drew tried to get in touch with her? How would she handle that?

Would she ever be able to truly rest and give up her guilt?

Drew didn't believe he was the father of a little girl and had denied signing any papers to acknowledge that. He had given up any legal paternal rights.

Josie prayed she'd never see him again, and she thanked *Gott* that Dinah was safe and happy.

But on sweet warm afternoons such as this one, Josie longed for the arms of another man. The boy she'd left behind in her shame and misguided confusion.

Tobias.

"I will walk you home."

He'd told her that the first day they'd met by a rocky stream that flowed down the mountain. By the time their walk home was over, Josie had a huge crush on Tobias Mast. After that, they had managed to find each other at singings and frolics. He had smiled at her the first time she went to a youth gathering after church.

Sitting across the table from each other after they'd sung lively hymns had soon become her favorite part of attending church. She knew she'd see Tobias there.

"I will drive you home."

Drive her home in his buggy? That was

a big step but one she cherished. It meant he wanted to court her.

"I will allow that," she told him with a smile, her heart already lost to his beautiful deep blue eyes. His curling light brown hair always needed to be combed, but he smelled fresh and clean, like that mountain stream.

"I cleared it with one of the ministers and with your friend's family," he said. "Then next we will arrange for you to meet my *daed* and my *bruder*."

Josiah had allowed her to come to Kentucky, hoping she'd find a suitable husband. Maybe she had. But she'd been mad at Josiah for so long she didn't want to prove him right.

Yet she couldn't resist Tobias. "We will?"

"*Ja*. And since you have a *bruder* back in Ohio, I will ask his permission to court you."

"No," she'd said, causing Tobias to frown. "I mean—my brother is not concerned about me. I make my own decisions."

"Are you sure about that?"

"I am when it comes to you," she'd replied, being the flirty girl she thought the world needed. While flirting worked with Tobias, he always respected her. She loved him for being considerate and cautious. She *had* loved him completely.

Now her heart ached with missing him, with remembering his sweet laughs and his kind nature. They had planned a future together in Kentucky. But that future had been shattered the night her whole world had shifted and changed forever.

With the scent of honeysuckle surrounding her and the warm wind moving over the fields and valleys of Campton Creek, Pennsylvania, Josie closed her eyes and wondered where Tobias was at this exact moment.

Tobias Mast paid the taxi driver and turned to stare up at the place where he'd reserved a room for the week. The Campton Center had been recommended to him as a place to stay while he conducted some business here. He'd heard the center, which used to be a private estate, now served as a source of help for the Amish who lived in Campton Creek.

When he'd researched Campton Creek, he'd found the center online at the library back in Orchard Mountain, Kentucky. Tobias had immediately called the Campton Center and explained that he was Amish and he was looking to settle in Campton Creek. A nice lady named Jewel had talked to him.

"If you need a doctor, lawyer, room and board, a safe haven, advice and help on anything, we will find someone for you. That's what we're here for."

"I just need a place to stay for a while," he'd explained. "I plan to buy a home with land in Campton Creek."

"We have several places for sale," the woman had told him. "I'll print out the listings for you and have them ready when you arrive. There are some beautiful properties here."

Now that Tobias had arrived from Kentucky, he wondered at his sanity. He'd come to Campton Creek not only to buy a house and land, but to find the woman who'd broken his heart.

Josie.

Closing his eyes, he remembered Josie's beautiful brown eyes and her golden-brown hair. She'd broken his heart and he needed to find out why. Why had she left him two months before they were to be married?

He could never forget the first moment they'd met.

"Who are you?"

Tobias had turned from where he'd been fishing in a mountain spring that ran through the community. He saw her and smiled. Her dark hair shimmered a deep reddish gold in the spring sunshine. She wore a light blue dress and a white apron, her black cloak open since the spring day had warmed. Her black *kapp* sat squarely over her oval face, its strings dangling against her neck. Freckles danced across her nose.

He went back to his fishing. "Who is asking?"

"I'm Josephine Fisher. I came here from Ohio with my friend. I might stay here."

He thought he heard a challenge in that declaration.

"*Ja?* Well, I'm Tobias Mast and I live here in Orchard Mountain. Why haven't I seen you around?"

She twisted the loose black ribbon of her head cover. "I have only been here for two days. I decided to come on a walk by myself. The woods are so pretty." She lifted her hand. "I love the wildflowers."

Tobias threw out his line and glanced over at her. Mighty spunky to take off into the woods alone. "Don't they have woods and wildflowers in Ohio?"

Her dark eyebrows lifted. "Of course. But I don't like Ohio."

Tobias gave up on the fish since talking to her seemed so much better. After they had sat on some rocks and chatted a while, he said, "I will walk you back home."

"I didn't ask you to do that."

"I want to. I am headed that way."

"Do you know the way to where I'm staying?"

"Not yet. But I will. *Wilkum*, Josephine Fisher."

She'd given him a big smile that had enveloped his heart. "You can call me Josie. Everyone does."

Josie. He'd fallen for her that day and he still loved her.

Now he'd tracked Josie back to the place where she'd grown up. They had been in love, so why had she left?

He needed answers. He'd stick around until he had them.

After his father's death, Tobias had inherited the family land and home back in Kentucky, but with both his parents dead and his only sibling living in Indiana, he'd decided it was time for him to move on. He sold out and packed a bag the day he deposited the check. After wiring his brother half of the asking price, Tobias had set out for Pennsylvania. Because he was alone and hurting, Tobias only wanted to find Josie and get to the truth, something he'd put off to stay with his ailing father. He couldn't move on with his life until he at least had the opportunity to confront her.

After that, he'd decide how to handle his future. If Josie was here, Tobias aimed to buy a place and settle in Campton Creek with the hope that she'd settle with him.

If she didn't want him, he'd still be near her, and that had to count for something.

Tobias walked toward the big brick home with the impressive columns on each side of the front door. All around, various trees heavy with spring sprouts hung like green veils. Garden trails wound their way around the grounds, annuals and perennials shouting in hues of red, blue and orange. The side yard held a parking lot complete with buggy hitches and horse railings.

That made him smile. Seemed this place did accommodate the Amish. He wondered about this obviously historic house and the Camptons. This town had obviously been named after the family. Tobias loved history and often checked out historical fiction or biographies from the library. Most of his friends frowned on such notions, but he liked to know about things.

His *daed* used to tell him that his curiosity would get him in trouble one day. Maybe so. Right now, he was curious about a clean room and a good meal.

Tobias rang the doorbell and waited.

An older woman with a bright smile on her face opened the door.

"Jewel?" Tobias asked, taking in her white hair and serviceable skirt and blouse.

"No, I'm Bettye," the woman said with a wave of her hand. "Jewel is our new manager, but she had to run some errands. You must be Tobias Mast."

"Yes, ma'am," he said, mindful to speak in *Englisch*.

"C'mon in, then," Bettye said. "I'll get you signed in and show you to your room."

Tobias took in the opulence of the estate house. "I appreciate that. I'm mighty tired."

Bettye checked the register on a small electronic pad, her fingers moving with haste over the keyboard. "Now, Tobias, we serve breakfast to our visitors at seven each morning. And if you ask ahead, we'll leave you some dinner on the stove."

"You must stay busy," he said, liking Bettye's calm demeanor. "From what Jewel told me, this place is truly a community center."

"Oh, I don't normally do much these days," she replied. "I'm a companion to the owner, Judy Campton. I was her assistant for years after my husband passed. When Admiral Campton died, she and I moved into the apartment over the carriage house. We usually have lots of people moving through here, but it's the end of the day. Jewel will be back soon. She lives here now and keeps watch over Mrs. Campton and me." Chuckling, she whispered, "They all think we're old, you know."

Grinning, Tobias followed her to the stairs while she continued. "The kitchen is located in the back of the house. You'll find snacks and drinks on the sideboard in the dining room. We have one of those newfangled coffee makers that use pods."

Tobias had seen those in his travels and marveled at how the machines made a cup of coffee from a tiny round plastic pod.

"My *daed* frowned on such notions," he admitted. "I think they're amazing, but I'm not supposed to admit that."

"I won't tell," Bettye said. They reached a door on the second floor. "This is your room. It has a small bath and a desk and chair. There is a table where you can eat if you'd like or you're welcome to eat in the kitchen or out on the sunporch."

Bettye turned to smile at him. "We operate from six to six around here, but if you need anything, there is a button on the phone that will ring through to Jewel. She's a light sleeper, and I must warn you—the woman used to be a bouncer at a nightclub."

"Denke," Tobias said, thinking Bettye was one of the kindest women he'd ever met even when she was warning him to mind his manners. "I think I will fall straight to sleep once I get settled."

"Oh, one more thing," Bettye said as she gave him a key card to his room. "Jewel left you copies of the real-estate listings she mentioned on the phone."

"I'll look those over," Tobias said. "I appreciate her doing that."

Bettye gave him a motherly stare. "Do you plan to buy land here?"

He nodded. "Yes, I do."

He didn't tell Bettye that he also planned to find Josephine Fisher. That was something he had to do in his own way and on his own time.

Once Tobias was in his room and had freshened up, he ate one of the cinnamon cookies along with a bottle of apple juice he'd found on the small wooden table.

Then he sat down in the comfortable chair by the window that looked out over a small side garden full of roses and some pretty shrubs, so he could read the listings he'd found on the desk.

Four different farms for sale. He skimmed the first three pretty quickly. He couldn't afford two of them and the other one looked in bad shape.

But the fourth one caught his attention and had his heart pumping too fast.

The Fisher place. Located next to the Bawell Hat Shop and Farm. The same address Josie's friend had given him. The directions were listed along with the price. Within his budget.

Was this the house Josie had lived in when she was young?

Chapter Two

The next morning, Josie saw her brother, Josiah, approaching the back porch of the *grossmammi haus*. He often stopped by after he made the rounds to tend the animals and take care of the milking.

"*Gut* morning," Josie called, smiling at her brother. Hard to believe she'd treated him so terribly after he'd found her in a local hospital sick with pneumonia just a few weeks after she'd left Dinah on the Bawells' porch. He'd brought her home to recover but it had been a hard road, both spirtually and emotionally.

"*Gut* day to you, sister."

Josiah's smile said it all. Her brother was at last happy and thriving after many years of being a nomad, tormented and in despair. They'd both been scarred by an angry, abusive father who'd treated their mother and them so badly that Josiah had left as soon as he turned eighteen. Josie had blamed him for leaving her there alone.

But he'd never given up on her, and he'd taken her to Ohio with him after their parents died.

He settled on the porch steps and stared out over the green pastures and the cash crops he'd planted to harvest this fall. Then he turned to her. "Josie, I need to tell you something."

Josie's heart jumped and skidded. She'd always felt that one day, Naomi and Raesha or her brother would tell her it was time for her to leave. Silly, but she couldn't get comfortable even though she felt safe here.

Putting a hand to her heart, she stared at

her brother. "What? Is something wrong? Did I do something?"

"Josie," he said, his hand reaching up to touch hers, his dark eyes bright with concern, "you are safe here and you have a home here, always. How many times do I have to tell you that?"

"I try to believe," she said, glancing around. "I know *Gott* brought me home, but I don't want to be a burden."

"You are not a burden," her brother said, shaking his head. "You have been a blessing to Raesha and me, and especially to Naomi."

"I love her." That was true even if at times Josie felt she'd been put with Naomi so the older woman could keep an eye on her. But Naomi had been nothing but loving and kind. They were quite a pair once they got going.

"We all do." He glanced toward the house. "Having you here to be a friend and helper for her means so much to Raesha and me. Naomi loves you as one of her own."

Josie bobbed her head and blinked away tears while she managed to calm herself. "I should not doubt. I will continue to pray and show grace and thankfulness." Wiping at her eyes, she asked, "So what do you need to tell me?"

"I have someone coming to look at the house today."

Josie shifted her gaze to the old homestead that she saw every day. Her brother had come back to Campton Creek and worked hard to restore it after a terrible fire had killed their parents years ago. A fire she'd felt responsible for starting. "Really?"

"*Ja.*" Her brother paused a moment. "I wanted to make you aware. Will you be all right if they want to buy our old home?"

"I don't mind anyone living there," she said. "I just can't go back there again."

"I understand," Josiah replied, his eyes kind. "But remember, the fire was an accident. You were a child, Josie. A frightened child who'd seen our father abusing our mother over and over again."

Josie closed her eyes, remembering how she'd accidentally dropped a lit lamp when she'd run into the barn to help her mother, to save her mother from their father's brutality. "It still hurts, *bruder.* I dropped the lamp and the hay caught fire and… Mamm screamed for me to run. They didn't make it out. It will always stay with me."

Josiah patted her hand. "But you're safe, and if we do sell, you'll have part of the payment for your future."

"I don't want it," she said on a sharp tone.

Josiah pulled away. "It's okay. We don't know if this man will buy the place."

Raesha came around the corner, carrying Daniel in her arms. Josie had not liked Raesha when she'd first been forced to come and live here. Now she considered her a sister.

"Here you two are," Raesha said, her gray eyes always gentle, her brown hair neat underneath her *kapp.* "Josiah, I'm off to the shop. Daniel will keep me company in the store today since he's fussy."

"Where is Dinah?" Josie asked, always one thought away from worrying.

"She's with Naomi and Katy Carver. Katy will take care of her but you can check on her for me, *ja*?"

Josie gave Raesha a soft smile. "I will do that. I can come and help with Daniel, too. And do whatever you need."

"Denke."

Katy, a couple of years older than Josie and a friend, often sat with Naomi and read to her while Josie helped in the shop. Josie loved Dinah, but she kept her distance, afraid she'd love her too much, so much that she'd want her child back one day. Just being near Dinah brought her happiness, but Dinah clung to Raesha and Josiah, the only parents she'd truly known. Josie could not force them to give Dinah back since she had no means of taking care of her daughter. Dinah would never know the truth.

Josiah stood. "I'm going over the foot-bridge to meet our potential buyer."

Raesha gave him a quick kiss. "I hope this one will stick." Then she glanced at Josie. "How do you feel about this?"

Josie swallowed her fears. "I hope a *gut* family moves in and puts love back into that house."

Raesha patted her arm, and little Daniel grinned and reached his chubby fingers toward Josie. She grinned back and tickled his soft tummy. He was such a precious child.

Raesha kissed her son and then smiled at Josiah before hurrying to the far side of the big house, where the hat shop and factory covered the other half of the property.

"So do I," Josiah replied after his wife had left. "It will be nice to have that land off our hands and into the care of another family."

He gave Josie a reassuring smile. "We could build a fence."

"No need," she said. "Once it belongs to someone else, I think I'll feel a lot better."

Her brother accepted that as he strolled toward the footbridge. Josie stood to stare after him, hoping she'd spoken the truth. Could she finally let go?

Tobias stood in the yard of the house next to the Bawell place. He knew Josiah had married and he knew the Bawell name. Josie had often mentioned Naomi Bawell, the kind woman who'd been a big help to Josie at times.

He had not seen nor heard from Josie for over three years. She'd left him right after Christmas, in a bitter cold winter.

Then a friend back in Kentucky finally told him Josie had written to her and let her know that she was safe and back home. She'd asked Sarah not to tell anyone, but Tobias had managed to find out the truth when chatty Sarah slipped up and mentioned Josie.

Now he studied the house in front of him. It looked fresh and newly painted, two storied with a long wide front porch and several windows. A smaller house than most, but doable for a bachelor or a couple just starting out.

Josie had never talked about this place much except to say her parents were dead and her brother had left when he was young. She'd often mentioned her brother but she didn't want to talk about the past. She'd missed Josiah but he'd lived in Ohio back then and Josie didn't reach out to him. How did they both wind up back here?

This looked like a nice farm. But the bigger question was, why they had both left?

A fairly new barn stood behind the house. The property was only a few acres, but he didn't need much. He planned to continue his woodworking and also grow vegetables year-round to sell at market. The *Englisch* loved the farm-to-table trend these days, so they'd buy fresh vegetables in bulk. They called this organic. The Amish called it natural since they'd been living off the land for centuries.

He heard someone behind him and

turned to find an Amish man approaching. "Josiah Fisher?" he called.

The man nodded as he came close. "*Ja.* I own this property. I understand you want to look it over."

"I do," Tobias said, shaking Josiah's hand. "I'm Tobias Mast."

Josiah looked surprised, but he quickly hid it behind a steady stare. "Are you from around here?"

"No, I'm from Kentucky," Tobias said, wondering if Josiah already knew who he was. From what he remembered, Josie hadn't told her brother much about him, either. "Orchard Mountain, Kentucky."

"Orchard Mountain." Josiah stood back, his eyes filling with questions. "Did you know my sister, Josie Fisher?"

Tobias couldn't lie. "I did. I knew her well. I was in love with her."

The other man went pale and then turned stern. "That's what I was afraid of. And you came here to buy our place?"

Tobias nodded. "If I like it, *ja.* But you need to know one other thing. I also came here to find Josie. I need to know why she left me." Seeing Josiah's concern, he added, "I found out from a reliable friend that she's back here and living with you and your new wife."

The other man glanced toward the Bawell property. "She is here, but she won't like this."

"She *is* here?" Tobias asked to be sure he'd heard correctly. Hope hit against despair in his heart. "Is she okay?"

Josiah put a hand on his shoulder. "Let's go inside and talk."

Tobias wondered if Josiah would try to keep him away from Josie. But he'd find a way to see her, sooner or later.

He walked into the house and glanced around, letting his questions stay unasked for now. The small kitchen area and a living room made up most of the first floor. He saw an open door into a big room and figured that would be a bedroom. "You've done a lot of renovations."

"I did," Josiah said. He told Tobias he'd come home a few years ago to sell the house. "Instead, I met the widow next door...and we got married. You seem to have already heard that, though."

Tobias heard the hesitation in Josiah's words. "But?"

"I'm just surprised you're here," Josiah admitted. "I never expected this since so much time has passed."

"Why is Josie here?" Tobias asked, needing to know.

Josiah guided him to the back of the house and stared out the wide window that looked out to the barn. "She'll have to be the one to tell you about *why* she's here. That's all I can say other than she wanted to come home. It is not my place."

"But something happened?" Tobias said. "You know why she left me?"

Josiah whirled to give him a solemn stare. Running a hand down his beard, he said, "I will not talk about my sister with you. If you like the property, you can make an offer. But I warn you, I will have to tell Josie about this. If she does not want to see you, or if she disagrees with you buying this place, then I will not sell it to you. She's been through enough."

Tobias saw the concern in the other man's eyes. "I'll take the place," he said. "Name your price."

"You saw the asking price," Josiah retorted. "Are you listening to me?"

"Then I'll give you that price." Tobias turned to take another look at the new kitchen cabinets and the big worktable. "I hear what you're saying, but I'm not leaving until I see Josie."

"You might be in for a world of hurt," Josiah said. "Josie doesn't get out much. She likes to keep to herself."

"Why? Is she ill?"

Josiah shook his head. "She is healthy and only just now getting back to normal. It's not for me to say."

Tobias backed off. "I understand. But I won't give up."

Josiah shot him a look of admiration. "I can see that clearly. But you might be in for the fight of your life. She could bolt and run again, and I don't want that."

So Josie had been running away? From what? Or maybe from who?

"I don't want that, either," Tobias assured him. "But I do want to buy this property, and one day I hope to get some answers." He shrugged. "Even if Josie never sees me or acknowledges me, I'll be here. Right here, watching over her and waiting for her."

Josiah nodded, appreciation in his eyes. "I pray that she'll see the good in you and accept your presence. She could use a friend, someone she can trust."

"She trusted me once."

"*Gott*'s will, she may again," Josiah said. Then he turned to leave. "I will let you know if I can accept your offer, Tobias. But don't hold your breath."

"I've been holding my breath since she left me," Tobias admitted. "I've got nothing but time."

"You're welcome to look around all you'd like. You can lock the door behind you."

"*Denke,*" Tobias replied.

After Josiah left, Tobias went to the corner window and stared out across the land. Josie was right next door, in that big house. So close, but so out of his reach.

Could he win her back?

Or was she too far gone to see that he still loved her?

Chapter Three

Later that day, Josie waited in the living room with Naomi. She wanted to find out if Josiah had sold the house, but he'd been busy all day long and she'd helped Raesha with the gift shop that served as the store-front for the hat shop. Spring brought in more tourists who wanted to buy home-made breads and jams, goat-milk soaps and lotions, and, of course, hats. So they'd barely had time to grab a sandwich in the back for dinner.

Now she was tired and hungry but also worried. She needed to remember what she'd learned in counseling. *Don't borrow trouble. Live in the moment and try not to project too many worries into the future.*

And trust in God.

"Should we head over to supper?" Naomi asked. "You know it's a treat to eat with the entire family when we can."

"We'll go in a moment, Mammi Naomi," Josie said. "I thought Josiah would come here first to talk to me."

Naomi's eyes had grown weak over the years, but Josie could tell the older woman was staring a hole through her back. "Child, you need to stop fretting. The house will always be there, even if someone else moves into it."

"But someone else could be happy there," Josie replied, touching a hand to her *kapp*. "That would make me very happy."

"You are so sure about that?"

She whirled to look down at the woman in the chair. "I believe I'm sure, *ja*."

"Sit and let us discuss this," Naomi said, used to Josie's rants and nervousness. "You are troubled by this news?"

"I'm worried," Josie admitted. "What if they aren't happy? What if that house makes them...not happy."

"A house has no power, young one," Naomi replied on a soft note. "A home has the power of love and grace and forgiveness."

"I want those things—in that house," Josie said, pointing a finger toward the window. "I need to know that, but my family didn't have those things."

"Josie," Naomi said, her smile serene, "you are right. You didn't have much grace and forgiveness, but your *mudder* loved you both so much. Now you have your *bruder* back and you have family right here in our home. So you have found love and grace and forgiveness, ain't so?"

"It is so," Josie said, turning back toward the woman who had always loved her. "I'm trying to live each day to the fullest, but today has been a difficult one."

"You are doing your best, child."

Naomi lifted slowly to stand. Josie moved the walker close so they could go to their middle-of-the-week supper with Josiah and Raesha. Usually the *kinder* were already in bed on these nights, probably because Josie couldn't bear to be around Dinah too much. She'd made progress, but it was hard. She appreciated that her brother and Raesha didn't demand she get more involved with Dinah. Holding the child for too long only made Josie sad for the past she'd lost. Would she ever be able to love anyone again?

"The sooner we get to supper, the sooner we can hear what Josiah has to say," Naomi pointed out.

Josie gave Naomi a wry smile. "You are the old, wise one."

Naomi chuckled. This was a joke between them. Old and wise versus young and confused.

"I am that," Naomi said, "but you are becoming more mature and wise by the day. I am proud of you, Josephine."

Josie let the sweetness of Mammi Naomi's words flow over her. "I will try to be worthy of your praise."

"Then help me get to my supper," Naomi retorted with a playful grin.

Josie helped her out the door and across the breezeway, the soft early-evening wind flowing over them with a feather's touch. Josie couldn't stop herself from glancing over at the house that haunted her dreams. The tree line blocked most of the house and barn, but she could see the corner of the front porch where she used to sit and play with the rag dolls her *mamm* had made for her. Josiah should have come to tell her if they had a buyer or not. But he'd busied himself all day with things that seemed suddenly urgent. He hadn't even stopped by the shop to see Daniel and Raesha.

Was he afraid to tell Josie that someone had made an offer?

Or maybe he didn't want to disappoint her if the place had not sold.

When they reached the back door to the main house, Josie turned once again to glance at the Fisher house. She saw a man standing on the porch in the very spot where she used to hide and play all by herself. The man looked toward her.

A man who seemed familiar. Just her imagination, Josie told herself to calm her jittery heart. She'd had Tobias on her mind and in her dreams for a long time, so it stood to reason she was now seeing him when he wasn't the one standing there.

Maybe Josiah had sold the place and he'd already turned the farm over to the buyer. Why else would someone be back there this late? And why did her heart skip and jump from seeing the man standing there?

After they'd made their way to the kitchen of the big house, the smell of chicken potpie wafting toward them, Josie saw the look that passed between her brother and Raesha.

Something was going on. She'd have to find out what exactly. The old dread resurfaced, making all her anxieties and doubts bubble up like boiling water.

Josie got Naomi settled, then went into the *bobbeli* room to check on Daniel and

Dinah. She did this when her fears started pulling her back into the dark.

Daniel slept away, his dark curls reminding her of her brother. She went to Dinah's bed and stared at the precious girl. Precious because Josiah and Raesha loved her so much, but hard to look at. Dinah only reminded Josie of the man who'd ruined her life. Her chestnut-haired daughter looked a lot like a Fisher, but Josie could see the markings of the *Englisch* boy who'd attacked her at a party. A boy who'd been Tobias's friend at one time.

I can't think about that now.

Naomi had taught her to pray when she was scared.

Josie stood by her daughter's crib and prayed that Dinah would always be happy and healthy and that she'd never know the truth of her birth.

Then she turned and went back into the kitchen to eat with her family. But now even Naomi seemed secretive and worried, her eyes holding Josie in a warm warning.

"What is going on?" she asked, her hands on her hips. "Josiah, what happened today?"

Her brother motioned to a dining chair. "Sit and let us eat."

Josie sat down and forced her fears away as they each silently said grace. But the silence seemed like an eternity to her.

When her brother lifted his head and opened his eyes, she said, "I can't eat until I know why everyone is looking at me as if I've grown two heads." Josie sank down farther on her chair and glanced from her brother to Naomi. "You know, too. All of you do. Please tell me if something bad has happened."

Naomi put a wrinkled hand over Josie's fingers and brought their clutched hands down against the table. "Your brother will explain and then we'll have our supper."

Josiah sighed and looked at his wife. Raesha nodded and took his hand. When he looked at Josie, his expression changed into a frown, his eyes filling with a dark doubt and then sympathy. "Josie, I showed the house to a man today and he wants to buy the place right away."

Josie let out a sigh of relief. "Is that all? Well, that's *gut*. Does he have a family? Is he from here? I saw someone over there as we were coming over. He looked familiar. Who is it?"

Raesha's eyes were wide, her expression quiet and blank. Naomi still held to Josie's hand. But now Josiah would not look her in the eye.

Josiah looked down in a hurry and then lifted his head, his eyes meeting hers. "It's Tobias, Josie. Tobias Mast. He's come to find you and he wants to buy our place."

Josie's heart stopped.

Her mouth fell open as she stared at her brother. "What?"

Raesha got up, came around the table and touched her shoulder. "It's true. He found out you are here and he wants to buy the property. But, Josie, you don't have to ever see him if you do not feel so."

Josiah nodded in agreement. "I told him

as much. I also told him I will not sell to him if you disapprove or feel uncertain."

"Feel uncertain?" Josie pushed her chair back and stood. "I feel so much more than uncertain, *bruder*. The man I was supposed to marry is here? It's been over three years since I left Kentucky. Why did you tell him that I am here?"

"I didn't," Josiah said, his eyes dark with regret and sadness. "He already knew. A friend of yours told him."

Josie should have never written to Sarah Yount. But Sarah had been her best friend since the day she'd arrived in Kentucky. They'd shared a lot of secrets, but Josie had not shared her worst shame even with her best friend. Josie had often wondered if Tobias had wound up marrying Sarah. Apparently not. Or worse, what if he'd brought Sarah here with him? But then, if he were married already, he wouldn't be here and demanding to see her.

She shook her head, her hand to her heart. "I cannot see him. I cannot. He shouldn't have come. I do not want him to live next door, Josiah. How could you even think that?"

Josiah rubbed his hand down his beard and looked helpless. "I was caught off guard and surprised. I wasn't sure what to tell him, honestly."

Raesha nudged Josie to sit down. Then her sister-in-law served the meal, the tension in the air as thick as the steam from the chicken potpie. Only Josie couldn't eat.

Josiah tried to eat his food but finally put his fork down. "I told him you wouldn't like this. He only wants to know why you left."

"He can't know that." Josie's eyes watered and she put her head in her hands. "What am I to do? I do not want to leave."

"You will not leave," Naomi said, her voice commanding and firm. "You will not go back out into that world. You need to be here, where we love you and understand you." Then she twisted to give Josie her full attention. "I need you here. We all do. And you need us."

After sighing and sitting silent for a moment, Naomi continued. "We will sleep on this and pray on it, of course. Your *bruder* has been trying to rid himself of that place for years. *Denk* on that. You have to let it go, too, and this might be the best solution, for so many reasons."

"I want to let it go," Josie said, trying to keep her voice calm. "But I don't need to *think* about this or wait until tomorrow. We cannot sell the house. Not to Tobias, of all people. Why would he even want it?"

Josiah looked at Raesha and then back to Josie. "He came for you, Josie. He wants you back."

Josie stood again, her whole body shaking. "Well, we all know I am not fit to be around him, let alone be his wife. That will never happen. He cannot live next to us. That cannot be."

She turned and ran out of the room and out onto the breezeway. The late-day wind lifted at the strings on her *kapp* and cooled her burning cheeks. Then she whirled and watched the setting sun shoot its last rays across the green land. The beams of light hit the house behind the tree line with a creamy-golden glow that hurt her eyes with its beauty.

At that moment, it seemed as if God had just touched his hand to the house that had been her prison and now was part of the yoke of shame she could never shed.

Josie stood watching the house, her mind whirling with a warring dance of both pain and joy. Tobias was here in Campton Creek, and he'd looked straight at her just a few minutes earlier. She *had* seen *him* there on the porch.

Her brother's words came back to her. *He came for you, Josie.*

But she couldn't let the joy from those words take over the pain that fractured her heart.

Tobias Mast might think he wanted her back, but if he knew the truth, he would turn and leave and she'd never see him again.

And if he stays, she thought, wondering

what that would be like, *would he even see me then?*

No. She would not give in to the need to rush over there and call out his name. She would not give in to the love she still held in that secret place in her heart. Love for a man who would be ashamed and embarrassed to be around her.

Josie watched the sun fade away and the dusk settle into muted grays as a hush came over the land. The house next door became a dark, looming shape that made her catch her breath and turn away, tears falling softly down her face.

From inside, she heard Dinah cry out, "Mamm. Mamm."

Heard that sweet voice while her eyes held to that looming shape in the darkness.

Josie sank down on the floor and cried the tears she'd been holding back for so long. The last time she'd cried like this was when her brother had found her inside that empty house with Dinah in her arms. She'd planned to take her baby and leave again, but Josiah had forced her to tell him the truth. She'd always believed she'd caused the deaths of their parents in the barn fire.

But Josie knew in her heart that her mother wanted to run out of the barn with her.

Only their father had held Mamm back. He'd held her back, and Mamm had cried out, her arms outstretched to her child.

Josie's arms were now wrapped against her stomach as the gut-wrenching pain of hearing her daughter's cries only mirrored her own cries as she saw her mother's tormented face surrounded by fire. How she longed for Tobias at that moment. She'd never told him what had happened that horrible day. Now she would never get that opportunity.

"What am I to do now, Lord?" she called out in desperate prayer. "What am I to do?"

Her whispered prayer lifted up into the night and disappeared into the emerging stars. A crescent moon hung bright and dipping just out of her reach.

Everything was always out of her reach.

Her baby. Tobias. Her mother. She could never have any of them back.

Raesha came out onto the porch. "Josie?"

Josie wiped at her eyes and lowered her head. "I am here."

Raesha sank down beside her and took Josie into her arms. "*Gott*'s will, Josie. *Gott*'s will."

Josie knew she should believe that and let things take their course, but how? How did she do that when the man she'd loved, the man who'd promised her a good life in Kentucky, was now here and he still wanted her?

She lifted up and looked at Raesha. "How do I find my way? Tobias will not accept me once he knows the truth. How am I to survive with him living so close? How?"

Raesha wiped at her own eyes. "We will be here to help you. This could be a *gut* thing. Tobias came all this way to find you, so he must still love you very much. You can take your time in deciding, but... what if you were honest with him?"

"He'll leave again and I will have to live with yet more heartache. I do not think I can bear any more, Raesha. No more."

Raesha stroked Josie's damp cheek. "And yet you'd send him away without knowing what might have been. What plan *Gott* has for you and Tobias."

"I thought my plan was clear. To be content and safe here with Josiah and you, Naomi and... Dinah. Little Daniel, too."

"You are safe. We will not let anyone hurt you again. You know that is your brother's only wish."

"Tobias could hurt me."

"Or he could heal you, Josie. He could heal you."

Josie lifted her head and glanced at the darkness. "I never imagined I'd see Tobias again."

"God imagined it," Raesha replied. "He knows your pain. He wants you to find the peace you seek. His will always shows the way."

"So Tobias is here for a reason?"

Raesha nodded. "He came to find you, and he's willing to buy that house just to be near you. That's what he told Josiah."

"Just to be near me." She let that cover her like a warm blanket. "That might be all he will get if he lives right there."

"That might be enough," Raesha said. "Enough to see what could happen."

She helped Josie stand. "*Kumm* and try to eat some supper. Naomi is concerned about you."

Josie nodded and wiped at her tears. "I'm not hungry but I will try. This is a big shock."

"I understand."

"Is Dinah all right? I heard her crying out."

Raesha smiled. "She is sound asleep again. A drink of water and a kiss, and she went back to bed."

Josie closed her eyes to the pain that sharpened each time she thought of all the nighttime kisses she'd had to give up in order to give her child a good life.

How much more was she supposed to give?

When they came back inside, Josiah breathed a sigh of relief. Without a word, he touched a hand to Josie's arm. "I am sorry."

Josie nodded. "I did not mean to upset everyone." She turned to Naomi. "I will take you back. You must be ready for bed."

Naomi shook her head. "Finish your supper and then we will go through."

To appease them, Josie took a few bites of the potpie Raesha had kept warm on the stove. But the food stuck in her throat and she finally pushed her plate away.

Josiah almost said something, but his wife gave him a warning glance and he looked away. Raesha took her plate. "I'll finish up here. Leftovers tomorrow for dinner."

Josie hugged her brother. "I will consider this and we will talk later. I do not know what I will do."

Josiah nodded, his dark brown eyes wide with worry. "Sleep, sister."

Josie doubted sleep would come. How could she shut her eyes without seeing all the images she'd tried so hard to put out of her mind? Her mother's tears and screams. Dinah's cries and needs. Tobias the last time she'd seen him, their last kiss.

He had not known it was their last kiss. He still had hope.

"I cannot wait to marry you," he had whispered, his words breaking her heart as he talked about the new year coming. He went on and on about building a house, having their own land, how he'd continue with his woodwork and how he wanted to grow vegetables for restaurants.

Josie had only smiled and touched his cheek. "I love you," she'd said. "I love you and I know you will succeed with your dreams."

"I want to take care of you, Josie," he'd

told her. "I want you to have the best I can provide for you."

"I want that, too," she'd replied, her mind in turmoil over all she would have to give up.

Then she'd left in the middle of the cold, dark January night, her heart torn apart and a baby growing in her tummy.

A baby who belonged to another man who had assaulted her and used her without any qualms and left her drugged and drowsy without even remembering her name.

How could they ever reconcile with that between them?

Chapter Four

Tobias waited at the property the next day to see if Josiah Fisher would let him buy the place. A dark cloud hovered in the morning sky, threatening a good rain. But Tobias hardly noticed the weather.

The more he'd thought about things, the more Tobias felt God had led him here to this spot for a reason. A reason that went beyond starting new.

He wanted to go back. Back to the past and his life with Josie. They'd been happy and ready to get married. He'd had a solid plan to take over some of his father's land and grow produce to sell to the local restaurants. He'd gotten all the permits and studied up on all the laws regarding home-grown organic foods. He'd sell his wood carvings on the side, too.

Josie had approved all of it, and they'd laughed and planned their future. Until that January, when Josie had become quiet and pale, her moods shifting like the unpredictable winter winds. Something had been bothering her since before Christmas, but she refused to discuss it with Tobias. She kept telling him she loved him, her words almost desperate. What had she been hiding?

The last night he'd seen her, she had been so sweet, but almost sad. "I wish Christmas could have lasted forever."

"We'll have lots of Christmases together when we're married," he told her, his hand holding hers. He remembered how she trembled and stared out into the January sky.

"I would like that."

"You will have that. We will celebrate

all the seasons of life, Josie. I will always take care of you. Always."

She nodded, tears in her eyes. "I want that, too. To always be with you, Tobias. Only you."

She'd left him that January without any word of explanation, not even a goodbye note.

For the last few years, Tobias had wondered why she'd left and where she had gone.

Now she was so near but still far away from him. He thought he'd seen her last night with an older woman in a wheelchair. They'd moved along the open breezeway between the main house and the other smaller house behind it. A *grossmammi haus*, probably.

The woman he'd spotted had stopped and stared for a brief moment. Josie?

He stood now in almost the same place on the front porch of the Fisher house and glanced over at the neat, rambling Bawell property. A successful property with thriving livestock and a growing business.

Maybe one day he'd have that, but right now he only wanted to see Josie.

Overhead, lightning hit the sky and then thunder followed off in the distance. He'd get soaking wet trying to get to the taxi booth, but he'd needed to come back today to look this place over once more. He wanted to buy this house and land, and he felt that in an urgent way.

He watched as Josiah Fisher came out of the big two-storied white house next door and began walking toward him. Had Josiah told Josie Tobias had come to buy the land and that he wanted to see her?

Josiah met him on the porch, his expression as dark and grim as the sky behind him.

"She doesn't want me here, does she?" Tobias asked after seeing the sympathy in Josiah's eyes.

A soft blowing rain began and Josiah motioned to the empty house. "Let's go inside before we get soaked."

Tobias followed Josiah into the house,

hope washing away with each drop of rain. "Josie did not like my idea, *nee*?"

Josiah paced around the small living area and then went to stare at the kitchen sink and check the stove.

"You don't have to explain," Tobias said. "I understand if she's not ready to see me." Then he held up a hand to stop Josiah's pacing. "Did I do something to hurt her? To make her stop loving me? Is that why she went away?"

Josiah removed his hat and rubbed his head. "I'm sorry, Tobias. But I cannot hurt Josie any more. She's doing so much better now. She's healing and she has a *gut* life here."

Tobias went still with fear and dread, his hands clenching into fists. "Better? Healing? Was she ill?"

Josiah's eyes widened. "I have said too much. I only came to tell you that I can't accept your offer. I am sorry."

Tobias watched as Josiah started toward the door. "Why won't you tell me the truth?"

Josiah shook his head and tucked his hat close. "I can't."

Then he went out the door and ran into the rain.

Tobias stood inside the empty house, the dark skies all around him pouring out the grief he'd felt since Josie had disappeared.

"Why?" he shouted to the heavens. "Why did she leave me?"

When he heard the door slipping open again, he whirled, thinking Josiah had returned.

Instead, he saw a young woman standing there, wet and cold, shaking with a chill, her lightweight cloak and black bonnet soaked. She removed the bonnet and tried to adjust her *kapp*. Then she lifted her head and looked at him.

Tobias gasped, his gaze holding hers. "Josie?"

She stood against the wall, frightened and afraid. She looked different. More mature and world-weary but still beautiful to him. "Josie, you came."

She nodded but never moved from the

wall near the door. Clinging to her bonnet with both hands, she kept her gaze leveled on him. "I followed Josiah and hid until he left."

Her words were whispered and choppy. Was she afraid of him?

Tobias moved toward her, but she held out a hand. "Do not."

"I want to hold you, to touch you," he said, unable to stop the words. "I have missed you."

"You must leave," she said. "If you will not listen to my *bruder*, then listen to me. I do not want you here."

Tobias felt the sharp slap of her words so much that his eyes burned. "What did I do to you, Josie?"

"You did nothing," she said, her eyes wide, her stance firm. "You did nothing. I only came to make you see reason."

Tobias moved closer. "All I see is the woman I loved, the woman I still love. I want to buy this place. I *need* to buy this house. *Mei daed* is gone. Died about four months ago. I sold the land and came looking for you. I could not leave him, but now… I have no one left. I came for you, Josie. And whether I live here in this house or not, I am not going to go away until I get some answers. I will not leave you, no matter."

The woman standing before him started to cry. "You must leave, Tobias. It's over. It has to be over."

Then she turned and ran out into the rain.

He ran after her but stopped on the porch. He didn't want to frighten her. "Josie?" he called, the wind taking her name out into the trees. And taking her secrets with it.

Tobias stood there staring after her, his heart breaking all over again while the wind and rain lashed at his soul. Why had he come to this place anyway? Had he been wrong after all?

He watched Josie run across the arched bridge between the properties, watched and wished he could have held her close. She looked so tormented, so lost, her dark eyes misty and full of regret, her hands holding to the wall behind her.

Tobias made sure she made it home and saw her dart into the small house past the main house. So she did live in the *gross-mammi haus*.

She'd told him he'd done nothing to cause her to run away from him.

Thinking back over her words, Tobias had a realization. If he'd done nothing, then who had? And what had they done to make her so sad and afraid?

Josie couldn't believe she'd gone to see Tobias. But she had to see him with her own eyes to believe he was actually here. After so many nights when she'd dreamed of their time together and had imagined what their life could have been like if she'd stayed and married him, she had one fleeting moment that maybe her dreams could come true.

But that was not to be.

Now she hurriedly dried herself and put on a clean dress and apron, hoping Naomi had slept through the whole time she'd been out in the rain.

When she came out of her small bedroom, she saw Naomi waiting patiently in her wheelchair. "Oh, you're up," Josie said. "I'll start breakfast."

Naomi held up a wrinkled hand. "*Kumm* and sit here, Josie."

Josie moved to the chair near Naomi. "Are you all right?"

"I'm *gut*," Naomi said. "I am concerned about you. Why did you go out in the storm?"

Josie could not lie to Naomi. "I went for a walk."

Naomi nodded. "Oh, a short walk?"

Josie looked down at her hands. "I went over the bridge."

"Over the bridge toward your old home?"

She looked up at Naomi, tears forming in her eyes. "I had to see, Mammi. I had to know. He is here. Tobias was there in the house. Josiah told him he cannot buy the place. But...he still wants to do so."

"Did you speak with him?"

"Only to tell him he should go."

"What did he say to that?"

"He wanted to know what happened. He wants to stay."

"How do you feel about that?"

Josie let out a shuttered breath. "I don't know how to feel. I've pushed those feelings away and stanched them so tightly I can't open my heart again. Not to Tobias. Not to anyone."

Naomi sat silent for a moment, her head down. Sometimes she did nod off. Josie hoped this was one of those times.

But her beloved *mammi*'s head came up. "I have thought about this situation." Naomi reached for Josie's hand. "*Mei* dear, maybe you should tell Josiah to let Tobias buy the place."

"Why?" Josie asked. "Why would I want that kind of torment?"

"It might not be such a torment," Naomi said, her eyes full of compassion. "Tobias came all this way to find you and he wants your old home so he can be near you. That says a lot about his faithfulness and his mindset."

"He always was stubborn," Josie admitted. "He's set in his ways. When he wants something, he goes after it."

"So he wanted you once," Naomi said on a chuckle. "And he still loves you. That is a *gut* thing."

"It could be, *ja*, but he is still very angry and hurt. I cannot tell him the truth." Josie shook her head. "I do not know what to do, Mammi Naomi."

Naomi nodded. "I have one more question."

"Okay."

"What was the first thing you felt when you saw him there in your old home?"

Unable to deny it, Josie wiped at her eyes. "I felt joy and… I felt peace. A short sweet peace, as if I could finally breathe again."

"And then all the pain came crashing down?"

"Yes."

Josie got up and started breakfast, her

hands shaking as she measured oatmeal and poured milk.

Naomi rolled her wheelchair over to the kitchen. "Maybe you could concentrate on that joy and peace, knowing Tobias is nearby."

Josie finished cooking the oatmeal and measured out sugar and cream before adding some fresh berries. "How can I have joy and peace knowing the man I was supposed to marry is living alone in a house that I hate?"

She placed Naomi's food on the table and then sat down with hers. But her stomach recoiled and her heart beat a hurtful tempo. How could she find any peace now?

Naomi said, "Let us have a quiet moment with the Lord."

Josie closed her eyes and thought again about seeing Tobias this morning. He looked the same, only older, stronger and more mature. Beautiful. He was a beautiful, loving, kind man. The kind of man she'd always dreamed of marrying.

Would it be so bad to have him back in her life?

When she heard Naomi's spoon hitting her dish, Josie opened her eyes and saw the truth. She couldn't allow Tobias back in her life. He would not want her if he knew the truth.

Tobias went into the kitchen at the Campton Center, his mind on breakfast. He'd missed the early breakfast so he could meet with Josiah Fisher this morning, but that had not gone well. He'd been here three days now and he wasn't ready to give up yet.

Especially after seeing Josie. She'd grown even more beautiful since he'd seen her last, but she looked fragile. Like a delicate flower tilted in the rain. Tiny and dainty.

With a shattered shimmer in her pretty eyes.

Tobias stared at the fancy coffee maker, his mind still on Josie. The more he thought about it, the more convinced he'd become that something bad had driven her away from Kentucky. And him. Since they'd loved each other, he knew he couldn't have done anything to make her take such a drastic step. He aimed to find out more.

"That thing ain't gonna start up by itself."

He turned to find Jewel grinning at him behind her black glasses. After stepping forward, she pushed a button on the machine and brought it to life.

Jewel was an interesting woman. She wore her dark hair short and spiky, but she dressed in colorful full-skirted dresses or what she called tunics over bright pants. And her shoes were always a surprise. Flowery tennis shoes or painted boots. He never knew what she'd have on next. She changed during the day since, as she'd told him yesterday, "I wear a lot of hats around this place."

That was true. Sometimes she was the plumber and sometimes she was the cook. Others came and went, helping here and there. Lawyers, doctors, nurses, business-people, all willing to help people who needed their help. But Jewel ran the show.

He wanted to ask her who he could find to mend a broken heart.

Jewel nudged him. "See the light? That means it's ready for your pod."

Tobias blushed. "Sorry. I have a lot to think about."

"Did you find any property?" Jewel asked while she handed him a round pod of dark coffee. Then she opened the coffee maker and pointed.

Tobias put the pod in and shut the lid, then found a mug and hit the biggest cup size available. "I found the perfect place," he admitted. "But I can't have it."

Jewel found two muffins and motioned to the kitchen table near a big bay window that looked out over the sloping yard and the creek past the swimming pool.

"Sit, Tobias, and tell me your troubles."

"How do you know I have troubles?" he asked after he brought his steaming coffee over.

"Everybody's got something," Jewel replied in a sage tone, waving her hand in the air.

She wore intricate rings on each finger, so Tobias saw flashes of yellow, deep blue and a shimmer of red.

Tobias didn't know what to say, so he bit into his carrot cake muffin.

"Take me for example," Jewel said. "I went to juvie, had a bad rap sheet, mostly petty crimes, and I hated the world. Plain and simple."

Tobias lifted his eyebrows. "What's juvie?"

Jewel chuckled. "Juvenile detention center. In Amish speak, that'd be *kinder* jail."

"Children's jail?"

"Teenage and underage jail," Jewel said slowly.

"You were in jail?"

"I was. But once I got out, I decided I didn't want to go back. Thankfully, I met Judy Campton, and she told me I had potential but that I also had a thick noggin. I took her words to heart."

"You've known Judy Campton for a while, then?"

Jewel squinted. "About fifteen years now. Thanks to her, I worked hard and let God take care of the rest. I found employment here and there, waiting tables and taking on odd jobs while I got an education. Now I have me the best job in the world. I landed here and became manager about a year ago—and exactly when she and Bettye needed me, too. And I don't plan on leaving."

"So you like being in Amish country?"

"Love it," Jewel replied. "The Amish don't judge me and I don't judge them. It is a mutual admiration society."

Tobias shook his head. "You are one amazing woman, Jewel."

"And I'm a good listener," she said. "Judy taught me that when I listen, I can hear things."

Tobias wasn't so sure about that, but Jewel's logic couldn't be challenged right now. He needed help and she was willing.

"Don't give me that look now," Jewel

said, her big green eyes staring him in the face. "Talk to me."

Tobias polished off the other muffin and took a long sip of coffee. "I want the Fisher house."

"The one near the Bawell place?"

He nodded.

Jewel slapped his arm with a mighty force, causing him to frown. "Sorry. I'm just so tickled for you."

"As long as you don't try to tickle *me*," he retorted.

"Well, that wouldn't be proper. Now, tell me—did you make an offer?"

"I've offered everything, including my heart, but they don't want to sell to me."

"What? They sure do too want to sell that place," Jewel said, one hand grabbing at her short sprouts of hair. "Josiah and his sister left it empty for years. He came back and fixed it up and then got himself married to that precious Raesha. I know for a fact he wants to be done with that property."

"His sister doesn't want him to sell," Tobias said, his heart burning. "I mean, she does not want *me* to buy the property. She doesn't want me here at all."

Chapter Five

"Why not?" Jewel asked, her head lowered but those dark brows jutting up.

"It's a long story."

"I've got a few minutes."

Tobias hesitated, but Jewel gave him an imploring stare. "We're here to help, Tobias. You look like you need a friend."

He did indeed need a friend. So he poured his heart out to this strange, eclectic woman. Then Bettye and Mrs. Campton came down to sit in the sunroom, and soon they'd heard the whole story, too.

"I have worked with Josie," Mrs. Campton said. "She was in bad shape when she returned to us."

"Why?" Tobias asked.

Silence, then measured glances between Bettye and Mrs. Campton.

"Do you all know what happened?"

"I don't," Jewel replied, her eyes bright with curiosity. "Miss Judy keeps her secrets to protect those who are hurting."

"I don't know much," Bettye said, her eyes soft with concern. "But people talk and I do know that was not a happy house for either of the Fisher children."

"I can't reveal any confidences." Judy Campton grasped her pearls with a shaky hand. "You must understand Josie was lost and now she is found. She's doing much better, but she has a long way to go to be completely well and good."

"Why won't anyone tell me?" Tobias asked. "If I can't buy that place soon, I'm going to have to find somewhere to live or go to Indiana and live with my brother. He and I do not always see things in the same way. He blames me for Josie's leaving and I have no idea why she left."

Judy Campton held up her hand, a diamond solitaire flashing at him like a beacon. "If you want my advice, I'd say try again to buy the house. If that doesn't work, stay here and find work and a place to live. Josie needs you, Tobias."

"She did not seem that way this morning. She told me to leave."

"She also needs time," Judy Campton said. "I'd hate to see you give up when you could be the blessing she needs so she can have the life she deserves. Go back to Josiah and ask again."

Tobias filtered that advice, but he didn't think he'd ever get the answers he needed to win Josie back. "But if he says no, you think I should still stay in Campton Creek."

"Yes, and while you are here, you show Josie in a million little ways that you have staying power."

He looked at Bettye after hearing that tall order. "A million little ways?"

"Little ways can lead to big trust and great reward," Judy added to Bettye's advice. "And Josie needs to learn to trust again."

Jewel hit her hand on the table, startling all of them. "I told you, if I listen, I hear things. And I just heard good advice for you, Tobias. Be still and know."

"You heard that?" he asked, smiling.

"I did. Be still but take action while you're in a holding pattern. That's what Mrs. Campton just told you. The trust will come if she sees you ain't going anywhere."

Trust. In a million little ways. Be still and know.

Tobias had never been good at waiting, but he'd do it for Josie. For the life he still wanted with her.

"I will try your suggestions. *Denke*, ladies, for being so kind to me."

"That's our job," Jewel said, almost slapping him again, but thankfully she just chuckled. "And that's our hearts. We love people."

Tobias went to the phone on the wall near a small desk that had been set up for anyone who needed to use it. He called the Bawell Hat Shop and left a message for Josiah. He'd try once again to buy the Fisher property, and if that didn't work, he'd go to plan B. Finding a job and staying in Campton Creek.

Then he would have to start the countdown on a million little ways to make this work.

"You want me to lie to my sister?"

Tobias shook his head, hoping Josiah would see reason. "No. I want you to let me buy your old place as a silent investor for now."

"For now?" Josiah pulled at his beard. "What do you mean?"

Tobias glanced around the bench they had found when he'd called Josiah to meet him near the Hartford General Store. "I want the place and I have the money. Let me buy it but don't tell Josie."

"I cannot hide that from her."

"All she needs to know is—" Tobias stopped and sighed. "It's a bad idea, isn't it?"

"Ja," Josiah said with a smile of relief. "The worst thing you could do is lie to her and withhold information. She doesn't trust anyone these days and that would be a hard blow to her. Especially coming from you."

Tobias let out a sigh and stared at the big creek that ran through town. "I am at a loss."

"We all are at times."

"Could you at least hold the house for me if I make a down payment?"

Josiah sat silent for a moment. "I can do that. I will hold it for one month."

"Two?"

Josiah chuckled. "You do not give up, do you?"

"Not when I want something."

"I hope one day my sister will see the good in you, Tobias."

"I will make her see that I will not give up on her, either."

Josiah's smile held a bittersweet tinge. "I hope so. If you can win her over, the house is yours. If not, I'll refund the down payment in full."

After they'd worked out the details, Josiah left and Tobias walked along the street. Campton Creek was a beautiful town and everyone here had welcomed him with smiles and well wishes. Now he just needed a job and a place to live.

When he spotted a help-wanted sign in a furniture store, Tobias hurried inside. It was an Amish establishment where all the furniture looked handmade. When the bells on the door jingled, a muscular man came out from the back.

"Can I help you?"

"Ja," Tobias said. "I saw the sign. You're hiring?"

"We are," the man said. "I'm Abram Schrock. I opened this store about three months ago and I need experienced wood-workers."

"I have experience," Tobias replied. He explained what he'd done in Kentucky. "I do carvings and I can work with any tool. I've made everything from tables to chairs and cabinets and chests." He took a breath and added, "I also carve things—birds, flowers, butterflies."

Abram grinned. "I can see you are eager."

"I need a job," Tobias admitted. "I want to settle here in Campton Creek." He wouldn't tell Abram anything beyond that, but he sure hoped the man would give him work.

Abram nodded, his dark eyes full of questions. "*Kumm* into the office and we will talk."

Josie sat in the buggy, her *kapp* centered on her head and her eyes straight ahead. She did not like going out, but today she'd had no choice. Naomi was feeling bad and Raesha had to take care of little Daniel. He had a cold and had been fussy all week. Josiah had work to do in the fields, but he and Raesha would take turns checking on Naomi. That left her to do the weekly run to the Hartford General Store. At least Katy had readily agreed to drive her into town.

"It will be a girls' trip," her always chirpy friend had told her as she pulled her family's buggy up to pick up Josie. "Do not worry. I will take care of you, and if you get uncomfortable, I'll finish the shopping."

"You are a *gut* friend," Josie had told her as they took off. She hadn't told Katy about Tobias showing up. Most of the community knew very little about her past except that she had a baby out of wedlock and her family would raise the child. But no one here held it against her, and they did not speak of it to protect both her and Dinah. The bishop had made sure of that. Or so she hoped. Josie had gone before the church and confessed that she was an unmarried mother and that she'd made some bad choices. She was forgiven. But that didn't mean some might not talk.

What if Tobias heard something? Another reason for her to fret about him being here.

Katy kept reminding her she needed to forgive herself. No one knew the whole truth about her being attacked. She did not want that shame to hang over Dinah's head.

"You are quiet today," Katy said, giving her a sideways glance as they clopped along.

"I am enjoying the nice weather," Josie replied. She'd always loved being outside. Mainly because bad things had happened inside her home when she was young. She'd spent a lot of time outside and in the barn, until the day she'd accidentally set the barn on fire. Blinking, she shuttered those memories.

"It is a beautiful day," Katy said, taking a long breath. "*Gott* brings special days for special reasons."

"It is the season," Josie replied, used to Katy's philosophical side. "Late spring is always special."

"*Ja*, because *Gott* saved this day for us,

a day of renewal and rebirth as the land comes back to life. A sign that we need to do the same."

Josie shook her head and decided not to argue with Katy.

They were both laughing when she glanced at the Schrock Furniture Market and saw a sight that shook her to the core.

Tobias, walking out with Abram Schrock. Shaking hands with Abram. Smiling and nodding.

"Who is that?" Katy asked with too much interest.

Josie couldn't speak. Tobias glanced up and into her eyes, his expression as surprised as her beating heart.

"Are you all right?" Katy asked, glancing from Josie to the two men.

"Drive," Josie said. "And watch where you're going."

Katy shot one more look at Tobias.

While he never stopped staring at Josie.

After Katy tied the big draft horse to the hitching rail in front of the general store, she hopped down and waited for Josie. "Who was that?"

"Why would I know?"

"He looked at you, Josie, as if he knew you."

Josie glanced around. The furniture store was down the street from the block-wide general store. But she didn't see Tobias anywhere on the street.

"I will tell you on the way home, when we are alone."

"*Ja*, you will," Katy said, her tone firm. "You know you can trust me with anything, but you seem to have one more secret."

Josie stopped and turned back. "I think I should go home."

"*Nee.*" Katy held her arm. "You can do this. You need to get out more and this is important. Raesha and Naomi need you to help, and today that means stocking up."

Josie took deep, calming breaths and prayed she wouldn't have a panic attack. She had not suffered one in a long time, months maybe.

"Breathe in, breathe out," Katy kept telling her. "Remember your list. Study it. That will calm you down."

Josie managed to keep walking as she searched the aisles of the big general store to make sure Tobias wasn't waiting for her. When Mr. Hartford greeted them with a smile, she smiled back.

But inside she was shaking and wishing she could go back home. When would Tobias leave? Because she didn't think she could keep handling things with him so close. And she had to wonder what he'd been doing at the furniture market. He had always been talented with wood carving and making beautiful things. She still had a tiny horse he'd carved for her years ago.

Then the unthinkable occurred to her. Abram had been asking around for someone to help out in the store and the workroom out behind the store. Someone who had experience making furniture and carving wood.

Had Tobias taken that job?

* * *

Tobias stood in the sunroom the next morning, giving thanks that he'd found a job at least. And that he had two months to do a million little things to make Josie trust him again. And maybe tell him the truth about why she'd left him.

But he hadn't been so great at finding a place to rent or stay. He talked to Bishop King and, ironically, the bishop had suggested the Bawell place.

"They have been known for taking in travelers, relatives and anyone in need. I've seen a lot of folks move through that big house."

Tobias had lowered his head. "I cannot stay there, sir."

"Oh, and why is that?"

Then he had to explain to the bishop, who he knew would not repeat what he'd told him.

Bishop King nodded after Tobias opened up with what he was feeling. "I know of Josie Fisher. She is a kind woman who's been through a lot. The Amish don't talk much of such things, but we are learning that the best of us sometime have emotional issues."

"But you won't reveal what's bothering her to me," Tobias said, making it a statement.

The bishop shook his head, his beard swishing against his dark coat. "I will not. You know where we stand on such things."

"I do and I respect that, but it's frustrating since I'd like to help her."

"*Gott* will see her through, and you showing up here to become part of her life again could be part of that plan." The bishop kept his eyes on Tobias. "If you take your time and do things in a proper way."

"So everyone tells me," Tobias said on a chuckle. He sure hoped so. He prayed so. He'd listen, as Jewel had so sagely suggested, and hope the Lord would show him the way.

Now he wondered what to do about a living arrangement.

He'd checked the Campton Creek newspaper and *The Budget*, but he'd found nothing. He started his new job today, so he'd have to worry about this later. Jewel had told him he could stay in the little room upstairs for another week.

That didn't give him much time, but he couldn't stay here indefinitely.

Tobias drained his coffee and hurried out to get to work before the Campton Center opened for business. People came and went here during official hours and he didn't want to be in the way. At the center he'd met a lot of Amish going about their business.

Nodding to Jewel and the efficient lady lawyer who had an on-site office, Tobias went out the side door and started his walk to work. He took in the quaint town proper and noticed the park across from the creek. This was a nice place. Small but not too small, with a lot of Amish influence but the modern world out on the main highway.

He didn't want to find an apartment

away from the village, however. He needed to be near Josie.

The first thing on his list was to buy her a spring plant and have it delivered to the Bawell place. She could nurture the plant and watch it grow. But he went into the flower shop and didn't see the kind of flowers Josie liked.

He'd have to figure something out and soon. When he saw a crop of wildflowers growing near the park fence, he had his answer. After taking the flowers he'd picked back to the Campton Center to put in water until he could have them delivered, he saw Jewel. Together, they picked more flowers from the garden.

"I'll keep 'em fresh and I'll even find someone to deliver them," she told him. "I won't tell who sent them."

"I appreciate that. I think Josie will know."

Just one of the many ways he could show her he cared.

Would she listen?

Would she hear?

He'd do anything to be able to talk to her.

I only want to talk to her, Lord. I pray for understanding and guidance.

Tobias needed *Gott*'s will to also be his will. He could not fail. If for no other reason than that Josie needed someone to love her.

Chapter Six

Tobias entered the furniture market and took in the scent of wood shavings. The smells of cedar and pine had always brought him comfort. If his hands were busy, his mind would follow, and maybe he'd figure something out while he did an honest day's work. And maybe he'd sleep better tonight.

Abram greeted Tobias immediately. The man always had a smile. "Here is my new helper. Are you ready to get to work?"

"I am," Tobias said, smiling. "I have missed having work to do."

"That's the attitude I like," Abram said.

"But before we get started, would you mind taking this list over to the general store?" He handed Tobias a small piece of notepaper. "Mr. Hartford ordered some of the special chemical-free adhesive I use, and it should have come in late yesterday but it didn't. Would you mind checking on it?" Abram touched his left knee, rubbing his hand against it. "My gout is hurting something awful this morning."

Tobias had noticed yesterday he walked with a limp. "I will go and check," he said, familiar with nontoxic and chemical-free adhesive. Then he grew curious. "How do you manage all day on that bad leg?"

Abram tugged at his beard. "I don't, most times. That's why I need a good helper. My last two did not work out. I have good employees out in the work barn, but I need to train someone up, since I only have three girls and they are all married and have duties to their families. They each have *gut* husbands who prefer to farm instead of work with their hands. I need someone who sees furniture the way I do. Our furniture has always been an art form, made with pride here in the country we live in."

"Do you think I could be that someone?" Tobias asked, hopeful. He liked nothing more than cutting, sanding and priming wood. He worked with the wood, not against it. The wood had integrity. He hoped his work would, too.

"We shall see," Abram replied with a knowing grin. "Depends on how fast you can get to the store and back."

"I am on my way," Tobias said, laughing.

He hurried across the street, his heart lifting to know that he might have a chance to create beautiful, sustainable objects out of wood. He'd had so many plans for the home he and Josie would have shared if they'd married. Tables, rocking chairs, dressers and hutches, cabinets and wardrobes. Maybe a cradle one day, too.

Those plans would happen if he could win her over and they could finally get married. A big goal but one he was willing to work on.

He walked briskly, eager to get back and begin his training. When he reached the general store, he quickly pushed at the door and entered.

Only to find Josie standing at the counter with a paper bag in her hand. When she looked up and saw him, her face went pale.

She did not look happy to see him.

Mr. Hartford spoke to Josie again.

"Josie, you said you needed to return something that you bought yesterday?"

"Ja," she managed to say barely above a whisper, wishing with all of her heart she hadn't needed to come back here today. "I got the wrong yarn." She swallowed, tried to breathe. "Raesha needs light blue. This is too dark."

"Then we'd better remedy that," Mr. Hartford said with a chuckle. Seeing Tobias standing there, he said, "I'll be with you in a minute." Then he went to find the yarn she needed.

Tobias lifted his chin in acknowledgment and took one step forward, his eyes wide with surprise. "It is good to see you, Josie."

Josie looked down at the counter, unable to speak, her whole system shutting down. What should she do? Josiah had come with her today since he needed to pick up some feed out behind the store. This was only supposed to be a quick exchange.

Why had she gotten the wrong yarn? Probably because her mind was on the man now staring at her.

Josie looked everywhere but at Tobias. Her mind would never work the way others did. She'd been damaged, traumatized, shattered. Would she ever be put back together?

"You cannot even look at me?"

She lifted her head at those soft words. Tobias had moved closer. Close enough for her to see the pain in his eyes.

Swallowing, she closed her eyes. "I need to go. Would you tell Mr. Hartford I'll *kumm* back later?"

She rushed past him even as he reached out a hand to her.

Josie needed air and sunshine. She hurried around the building and searched for her brother.

"Josie?"

Whirling, she saw Tobias behind her.

He held out a bag to her. "Here is the yarn you wanted. Mr. Hartford said it was an even swap."

Josie took the bag, her hand briefly brushing Tobias's. *"Denke."* A shiver went down her spine. He smelled clean and fresh, and he looked healthy and muscular. "You seem well," she managed to croak.

"I am *gut*," he said, his eyes telling her he wanted to say more.

Before he could speak, Josiah hurried to them. "Josie?"

Josie spun toward her brother. "I have the yarn. I am ready."

Josiah shot Tobias a long stare, but said nothing. "Then we should head home."

Josie didn't know what to say to Tobias, so she turned and headed toward the buggy.

But she heard her brother's words. "Everything all right, Tobias?"

"*Ja.*"

She looked back and saw him turn toward the front of the building. He looked over his shoulder, his gaze holding hers, his smile soft and reassuring.

Her heart couldn't be sure of anything except how much she missed him. When she got into the open buggy, Josie sank against the seat.

"Did you talk?" Josiah said, his tone hopeful.

"Briefly." She wiped at her eyes. "Why is he still here?"

Josiah clicked the reins and started the docile horse toward home. "I heard he found work at the furniture market."

Josie glanced toward the market. "Abram needs a strong worker."

"So you are all right with that?"

"I don't know," she admitted. "If he is not buying our home, why is he still here?"

Her brother sent her a quick glance and then watched the road. "I think he came here for more than a house, Josephine."

Josie gulped in air. Tobias wasn't going away. Could there be some hope for them after all?

Josie couldn't stop shaking.

After Josiah dropped her off, Josie hurried inside the *grossmammi haus* and dropped the bag of yarn onto the dining table. Then she rushed to her room and sat down in the rocking chair to stare out the window.

"Josie?" Naomi called from her room.

Naomi had been asleep when Josiah had come by to ask Josie if she wanted to ride with him so she could return the yarn. She should have let him do that deed, but he'd been preoccupied with Daniel being sick and trying to get his chores done. Her brother was acting odd these days. He barely spoke on the way home, his eyes straight ahead and his expression bordering on a frown.

Probably because he wanted to sell the house next door and she'd asked him not to sell to Tobias. Seeing Tobias had upset both of them, no doubt.

Josiah had given her a worried glance, then taken off toward the barn to finish out the day's work. Maybe he felt bad about her running into Tobias. It wasn't her brother's fault that Tobias had shown up out of the blue. No, all of this was her fault. She should have left her husband-to-be a note, explaining that she had to leave. But she'd been so distraught she'd left Kentucky as soon as she could.

Josie got up and touched a hand to her *kapp*. Her hair had gotten long again. She'd cut it when she'd been hiding out, so no one would recognize her. Now it was coiled in a tight bun on top of her head. She wanted to tear at the cover and pull at her hair.

But she had to stay calm and try to get through this.

"I'm coming," she called to Naomi.

Gathering her strength, she hoped Naomi wouldn't notice how frazzled she was. "Are you all right, Mammi Naomi?"

When the older woman didn't call back, panic set in. Josie rushed into Naomi's room and hurried to the bed. "Naomi? Naomi?"

"Was der schinner is letz?"

"That's what I'm asking," Josie said on a sigh of relief. "I thought something was wrong with you, but instead you are asking me that question."

"I was worried when you had to go back to town," Naomi said. "How long did I nap?"

"About an hour," Josie replied while she straightened the covers and helped Naomi sit up. "Are you sure you're fine?"

"I've never been better," Naomi said. "Why do you fuss so?"

Josie sank down on the rocking chair that matched the one in her room, the soft cushions comforting her. "I'm sorry. I... I saw Tobias in town, at the store."

Naomi's squint widened. "I might need a cup of tea before I hear this."

Josie tried to stay patient. "Would you like me to bring it to you?"

"*Neh*. We will go into the kitchen."

Josie helped Naomi up and into her wheelchair, then pushed her into the kitchen. After making two cups of tea and bringing the cookie jar over so Naomi could have a snickerdoodle, she finally settled down beside Naomi.

"He came into the general store and... talked to me."

Naomi stirred sugar and cream into her tea. "Did you respond?"

"I tried. But I got flustered and ran out without the yarn."

"Oh, dear. Josiah won't like having to go back."

"No, I mean, I have the yarn. Tobias followed me and brought it out to me."

"He does sound like a kind soul."

"He looked *gut*," Josie said before she

could take it back. "He always had a soft drawl to his voice."

"That's the Kentucky in him," Naomi said, now wide-awake and intent. "Was he born there?"

"*Ja.*" Josie allowed the memories to roll over her while she nibbled at a cookie. "His parents were so kind. His mother died a few months after I got there. I think I helped him through that and that's what bonded us. He had an older brother who moved to Indiana. They used to fight a lot."

"Most *bruders* do," Naomi said on a soft chuckle. "Tell me more."

Josie needed to tell someone the things she'd held so tightly to her heart. "His *daed* was a sweet man. He welcomed me and allowed Tobias and me to walk out together. He was happy that his younger son had found someone."

"I'm sure he saw what a wonderful person Tobias had found."

Josie stopped and put a hand to her

mouth. "We were happy once, Mammi Naomi. We truly were."

Naomi nodded and reached for her hand. "I can see that in your eyes. You still love him."

Josie pulled away and stood. "I can't love him. And he can't love me."

"But it sounds to me as if you both still care about each other. You've never talked about Kentucky much—or Tobias, either, for that matter. Your voice softens when you're remembering him."

"He was the love of my life," Josie admitted, tears burning her eyes. "But...it can never be now."

"You need to be patient and you need to be kind to him, in the same way you were when he lost his *mamm*. After all, he has done you no harm."

Josie lifted her head and stopped her pacing. "You're right. Tobias has done nothing wrong. I shouldn't be angry with him."

"Not one bit. But your anger toward this other boy has caused you a lot of pain.

You can't hold that against the man who has come here to find you."

Josie realized she'd been holding on to that anger and it had turned her from kind to bitter. Why should Tobias bear the brunt of all her woes? She glanced at Naomi. "You've done it again."

Naomi took a big bite of her cookie and lifted her eyebrows. "Done what?"

"Tricked me into seeing the light."

"I only listened and commented as needed," Naomi said with the innocence of a lamb. "You figured it all out on your own."

Josie sat back down, a tremendous lightness making her smile for the first time in days. "I did, didn't I? I will be civil to Tobias when I see him. But… I will not love him again. That is over."

"Of course. Whatever you decide."

Josie started clearing away their dishes. "I've decided. I won't change on that."

"As long as you're considerate of Tobias and his feelings, too, I think you've made the right choice."

Josie took Naomi out on the porch to enjoy the nice breeze and the sunshine. While Naomi read the large-print Bible Josie had given her at Christmas, Josie sat on the steps and stared at the house across the way. Maybe she should tell Josiah it was okay for Tobias to buy it.

But no. She might have to tolerate him staying here and finding work, but she could not tolerate him living so close to her, in a house that had brought her only pain and terrible memories. While she watered the daylily bulbs she and Naomi had planted around the breezeway, Josie thought about Tobias again. Having him near did bring her joy, but her secrets shattered that joy with a piercing clarity. She couldn't change the past. But maybe she could learn better in the future.

Raesha came around the corner, carrying Daniel on her left hip while holding a bundle of fresh flowers in her free hand.

"There you are," she said, out of breath. "I came home with the *kinder*. He's even fussier today." Then she handed Josie the cut flowers. "Someone delivered these to the shop."

Josie took the beautiful flowers and sniffed at them. "Oh. Do you need me to put them in water?"

Raesha laughed. "They need water, but they aren't for me, Josie. The note had your name on it."

Josie looked down at the flowers in her hand, the paper covering part of the bundle. Lifting the stiff wrapping away, she smiled. "Dandelions, asters and trout lilies."

"Chickweed and daffodils, too," Naomi noted. "All so pretty with the yellow tones mixed in with the pinks."

"Who sent me flowers?" Josie asked. "They seem to be fresh picked."

Raesha and Naomi exchanged motherly glances. "There was no name on the note," Raesha said. "The delivery person wouldn't say who, either."

Josie sniffed the fresh flowers and then looked over at the house that seemed to watch her all the time. "My favorites," she said on a soft whisper. "I love yellow flowers the best."

And she knew of only one person who would go into the woods and find wild-flowers for her.

Tobias.

She knew it had to be him.

And so did the two women watching her so closely.

Chapter Seven

Tobias loved the smell of fresh-cut lumber. A fresh piece of solid wood was always a challenge for him. Each piece held a certain forest scent. His *daed* and older brother didn't mind him making furniture, but they'd frowned on him whittling tiny replicas such as animals to sell as toys. They also frowned on decorative stencils, but the *Englisch* loved that kind of thing, as well as distressed furniture.

He'd finished his first week of working for Abram, and while he'd enjoyed working with Abram, he still hadn't found an affordable place to live. Abram came out of the workshop and waved to him just as he was about to clock out. He intended to retrieve his suitcase from the Campton Center and move to the hotel at the edge of town.

"Tobias, could I speak to you?"

Tobias turned back up the main aisle that showcased gleaming walnut and oak headboards and nightstands along with rocking chairs and cradles. He'd made his first oak headboard this week and hoped it would sell. Oak was a strong, sturdy wood that would last a lifetime. Had he done something wrong? Forgotten to clean and put away his hammer and chisel? Overstepped by meticulously explaining the different woods to the other workers? Abram looked so serious.

"Yes, Abram?"

Abram tugged at his beard, a habit Tobias was beginning to get used to. "I hear from Jewel that you still need a place to stay."

Tobias nodded, thinking the worst. Abram had been willing to hire him even if he didn't have a permanent address yet. "I am looking. She said she'd ask around, but I didn't know she'd told you. I hope that is not a problem."

Abram checked the sale receipts and tidied the long counter where the clerks worked the cash register at the back of the shop. "She asked me because my wife and I have a big house and all of our children are grown and in their own homes. We have a bedroom on the far left side of the house that's near the back porch. It's big enough for a sitting area—my *mamm* stayed there when she'd come visit. But she passed about a year ago. You would have privacy there and you can come and go out the back as you like, and we won't bother you."

Tobias blinked. Abram lived on the other side of the community, away from the Bawell house. "You mean you'd rent the room to me?"

Abram's gaze showed sympathy and understanding. "Jewel told me about your need right after I hired you, but I wanted to get to know you before I asked. You're a *gut* man, Tobias. And I kind of enjoy that Southern accent of yours."

Tobias couldn't hide his smile. "I am glad to hear that."

Abram went on. "Rent would include breakfast every morning and dinner every night unless you have other plans. We'll feed you all you want."

"No. If I'm paying for room and board, then add a little more extra for meals," Tobias replied. "That's the only way I can accept."

Abram grinned and shook his head. "You drive a hard bargain by offering to give part of my money right back to me and add extra, but I think Beth will agree to that."

Abram named his price, which sounded reasonable. "I added a few dollars extra for meals, but if you start putting on weight, I might have to add more."

Tobias liked Abram, and this would keep him from wanting to go to the Fisher place when he had nothing else to occupy his time.

"Okay, I accept your kind offer." Tobias breathed a sigh of relief. "*Denke*, Abram, for everything."

Abram slapped him gently on the back. "We can swing by the Campton Center on the way home. And since today's Friday, you're in for a treat. Beth makes peach cobbler almost every Friday so I can have some for breakfast on Saturday. That'll include you now, too."

"That will be *gut*," Tobias replied, his stomach growling. He'd packed a lunch from leftovers at the Campton Center, but that had been gone hours ago. "It will be nice to have some good home cooking."

"Beth will feed you—don't worry about that. And you'll bring her joy, eating her food. She loves to bake, and she misses our daughters." Abram took off his leather apron and hung it on a hook behind the counter. "She loves when they bring the *kinder* to visit. Bakes cookies for days.

Especially at Christmas, when they bring their husbands, too."

Tobias missed his mother's cooking. He and his father had made do with what they could scrounge up and with the few casseroles and desserts neighbors brought by. He'd had many a young woman try to ply him with food, but while he appreciated the meals, he couldn't take things with any of them further than friendship. Which meant the homemade food that had started on a regular basis had trickled down to not much.

Nodding at Abram, he said, "I'll make sure and let her know how much I'll enjoy the meals, then."

Together they cleaned up and locked down the shop and the workshop. Tobias liked working here with Abram and the two other men who did everything from sawing and cutting to sanding and loading. But those two didn't have an inkling about creating something from wood, although they worked as hard as anyone. Tobias, on the other hand, had shown Abram some of his designs. Abram had immediately liked all of them. The slow pace of creating something by hand had always fascinated Tobias. Thankfully, Abram understood that need to create beautiful things.

Now, if Tobias could just get on with the other business of being here. He wanted to see Josie and talk to her, try to get her to open up to him. Would she allow that?

He wondered if she'd liked the flowers he'd sent. He had meant to send store-bought, but they looked so obvious and were way too expensive. Not that he minded the cost, but he knew Josie loved flowers straight from the earth. She'd planted herbs and sunflowers back in Kentucky. He could still see her running through a meadow of wildflowers, barefoot and free.

A lot different from the shell of her he'd seen recently.

Glad he'd picked flowers from the meadow near the park fence and that Jewel had helped him clip some of the beautiful blooms surrounding the Campton Center, he felt sure Josie would know they were from him. A perfect batch of fresh flowers.

Would his first gift please her? Or would it backfire on him?

He'd find out from Josiah.

And maybe he'd see her in church on Sunday. Abram had invited him, but he'd almost said no. Until he thought about seeing Josie across the way, sitting with the other women.

That, and getting back on track with God, made him decide it was time for him to get serious about the things that mattered in life—a home and a family.

He only hoped Josie would get serious about getting to know him again. He'd have to start from scratch and court her in a proper and considerate way. As impatient as he was, Tobias knew he'd have to take things slow this time around. Or he'd lose her all over again.

With that in mind, he went with Abram

to pick up his suitcase and other possessions.

Jewel greeted him with a big smile when he came down from his room. "Are you going to stay with Abram and Beth?"

"*Ja*, thanks to you," Tobias replied with a gentle admonishment. "I am glad to have a place to sleep. Not that my room wasn't comfortable, but it's time for me to move on."

Jewel held her arms open. "Bring it in. Right here."

Tobias laughed as she hugged him tight. The woman had a grip. But it felt good to be cared for and hugged.

Jewel stood back, her floral top making her look like a flower garden had exploded all over her. "You remember, now—we're here to help. You need to talk, you come on in and grab some of that fancy coffee and a cookie and have a seat. Your friend Jewel here will listen and get you on the right path."

"I will do that," Tobias told her. "And, Jewel, once I'm on my feet and have some extra money, I'll be in here with a donation every week."

"Ah, that is so sweet. I'm gonna pray for you and your girl, Tobias."

Tobias thanked her, and after telling Mrs. Campton and Bettye goodbye, he got back in the buggy. "Here, Abram. The women wanted you to send Beth some spice mix they made."

"Oh, she'll appreciate that," Abram replied after he set the small bag between them on the seat. "She uses fresh spice in everything she cooks."

As they rode along, Abram's white-and-gray Percheron trotting in a graceful fashion, Abram carried on small talk and pointed out some of the farms and landmarks along the way.

"See that bridge?" he said, pointing to the red beams of a wide covered bridge. "That goes over the deepest part of the creek, but it brought the Amish side of town together with the *Englisch* side. The early Camptons wanted it that way since they allowed the Amish to start a community here."

Tobias could see that. "Judy Campton is an amazing woman and so is Bettye Willis. Jewel seems to love both of them."

"You mean Jewel who apparently has no last name," Abram said, nodding. "An odd woman but a loyal one. She does love those two. They saved her, I believe."

"Yes, that Jewel," Tobias said, understanding why Jewel went by only one name. "She's been kind to me."

"We have a lot of great people around here and we all get along, thankfully. I hope you continue to meet everyone."

"I hope that, too," Tobias said. Then he decided to be honest. "Abram, I came here to buy a farm, and I have my eye on the Fisher place."

"Well, now," Abram said, shooting Tobias a quizzical glance, "have you made an offer?"

"I did and I've put up good-faith money, but I'd rather you didn't mention that to others, in case it falls through."

"I won't repeat anything we discuss," Abram replied, his expression solemn. "I will say it would be good to see that place up and running again. It's sat empty for so long now. Since the fire that killed Josiah's parents."

Tobias tried to hide his shock, but Abram caught it. "You didn't know. Of course, you wouldn't. A barn fire. A horrible accident."

Tobias let that soak in. "But Josiah is their son."

"*Ja*, he returned to fix the place up to sell, but *Gott* had other plans. Josiah fell in love with Raesha Bawell and they have two children. A sweet girl named Dinah and a son named Daniel."

Two children. Tobias wanted children. He and Josie had talked about having several. But Josie was living with her brother and his wife, alone and still single.

At least he could be thankful for that.

But was she still single because she loved him? Or was she alone because she didn't want to be with anyone?

He wanted to know more. "I hear Josiah's sister lives there with them, too."

"She does," Abram said, looking away. "She is a companion to Raesha's mother-in-law, Naomi. Both Raesha's and Naomi's husbands died—years apart—and the two women clung to each other. Josiah fell for Raesha." He paused, gave Tobias a strange glimpse. "Josiah found Josie and brought her home. She has been back now for about two years or so."

Tobias didn't ask anything else. Abram might become suspicious. But he had to wonder where Josie had been the year after she'd left Kentucky. Somehow, he'd have to find that out to understand what had happened to make her leave him in the first place.

Because sending her flowers was one thing, but trying to win her trust enough that she would tell him the truth would be a big challenge.

As the bishop had said, the Amish didn't discuss such things. But how many people in this community knew Josie's secrets?

* * *

Josie couldn't stop staring at the flowers.

She'd found a vase and placed them on the small dining table where she and Naomi ate most of their meals. Josie liked to cook and Naomi enjoyed coaching her. Sometimes Raesha would join in and they'd take the meal over to the big house so Josiah could test the food. Those times made Josie smile because she felt loved and a part of something, a part of a strong family.

She thought about Tobias. Did he have any family left? Josiah hadn't mentioned much about him beyond Tobias wanting to buy their old home. Why would he leave Kentucky and everyone he knew to come here?

Because you are here.

That voice in her head gave her hope, but Josie banished that hope before it could take hold of her heart. These beautiful, colorful flowers also gave her hope, and yet she remembered when she and Josiah were growing up. No flowers around the house and no cut flowers inside the house. Stark, sterile, plain. That was how their father had expected things to stay. No books other than the Bible, no magazines or even newspapers. Her *mamm* heard news only when she went to church, and even then, her *daed* frowned on idle chatter.

After Josiah had taken her to Ohio, Josie had delighted in the wildflowers that sprouted out of the earth in a field beyond their uncle's house. She had been afraid to pick any until Josiah told her it was okay to do so.

She always kept a small vase of flowers in her room there, and when she'd gone with friends to Kentucky, she'd done the same after she'd decided she didn't want to return to Ohio. Tobias learned of her love for flowers and he'd often supplied her with colorful blooming plants or fresh-cut flowers.

The same way he'd done today.

"Are you expecting those blossoms to

jump out of the water?" Naomi asked as she rolled her wheelchair to the table.

Josie whirled away from staring at the flowers, remembering their chicken-noodle casserole should be ready by now. "*Neh*, just trying to figure out who sent them."

"I believe you know the answer to that question."

"I think I do," Josie admitted. "But I can't be sure."

Naomi fussed with the white napkins on the table. "This man seems determined to win you back, Josephine. He's found work, according to what you heard and saw in town, which means he's staying here indefinitely. I don't think he'll give up on that house next door or on you, especially not on you."

Josie checked on the small casserole and took it out of the oven. "He can't have either."

Naomi waited, her hands in her lap, as Josie set the steaming casserole on the blue floral pot holder she'd placed on the table earlier. "So you won't consider asking him if he made this kind gesture?"

"I do not want to talk to him."

"You could send him a note."

"Are you trying to get Tobias and me back together?"

"I'm only telling you to mind your manners. We thank people for kind deeds. I know you love flowers. Apparently, so does Tobias."

"What if he didn't send the flowers? Wouldn't that make thanking him a problem?"

"I believe Tobias sent the flowers," Naomi said on a firm note.

Josie poured tea and sat down. Naomi lowered her head and said her quiet prayer. Josie tried to do the same. But how did she pray for two different outcomes? She wanted Tobias to go away. She prayed he'd stay.

Because one thing stood out for her. She'd resented Josiah for leaving her and her mother alone with their father. He'd come back for her only after their parents had died. But Josie had not been kind to her brother and she'd defiantly refused to return from Kentucky during her *rumspringa*.

She'd stayed there to make the point with her brother that she didn't need him, and because she'd fallen in love with Tobias.

But another thing shouted at her now: Tobias had been the only person she'd ever known who had become her champion, her protector, the one person in the world she could trust to never leave her behind. Tobias had planned a life with her, a life where they followed the tenets of their faith together.

But one night had changed all of that.

"Always," she'd told him.

"Always," he'd repeated.

And in turn, she'd had to leave him behind. She'd left, heartbroken and full of shame, but she knew she'd broken his heart, too, in doing so. And yet he'd found her and he'd come to her hoping they could reconcile. After all she'd done to him.

"Child?"

Josie lifted her head, her eyes open. "Sorry, Mammi Naomi."

"Do not apologize for spending quiet time in your prayers," Naomi said. "You have a lot to pray about."

Josie nodded and lifted the creamy noodles and chunky chicken to her lips. Naomi was right, as usual. She needed to pray about all of this and consider her ways. *Gott* had guided her back home, despite her sins and her mistakes. Maybe He'd guided Tobias back to her, too.

Now she just needed to figure out how to handle that without revealing her terrible secret. Because she couldn't tell the man she'd always love that one of his *Englisch* friends had drugged her and abused her in the worst kind of way.

Chapter Eight

Tobias sat by the window in the cozy room Abram and Beth had rented to him. The big window looked out on the pastures and valleys. He could see the peaks of Green Mountain off in the distance. Josie had often talked about Green Mountain and how her big brother would take her up the trails to the top.

Why hadn't she told him about her parents dying in a barn fire? Maybe the trauma of that had somehow caught up with her, since she'd returned here to heal.

He wanted to know what kind of healing she'd needed.

But he'd only hear that from Josie since this community was tight-lipped about gossip.

Sooner or later, he'd meet someone who didn't mind explaining things. But he prayed Josie would tell him the truth without anyone else passing false rumors.

Right now, he had to get to church. Abram and Beth had offered to let him ride with them. He needed church, and he held out hope he'd see Josie there, too. Would she smile across the aisle at him? Or would she run away again?

"Tobias, are you ready?"

"*Ja*, Abram. Coming."

Tobias headed out the side door and met them on the back porch. "It is a good day to worship."

"You seem in a good mood," Beth noted.

Tobias liked Beth Schrock. She was bubbly and jolly and never seemed to have a bad day. But she noticed things other people never saw. Such as how he'd been moping around all weekend.

"I am feeling hopeful," he admitted. "I

like it here. Pennsylvania is a beautiful state and this is a good community."

Beth adjusted her bonnet. "Then church is a good place to start."

He offered to drive the buggy and the happy couple immediately agreed.

"You are spoiling us," Abram said from behind him in the open buggy. "First, you walk into my shop and show me the kind of talent a furniture maker only dreams of. Now you help me with the milking and get up before I do to feed my chickens and goats. And Percy there—" he pointed to the high-spirited Percheron "—seems to think you're his baby *bruder* or something."

"He has indeed taken a shine to you, Tobias," Beth said in agreement.

Tobias laughed over his shoulder, then turned to watch the narrow paved lane ahead. "Percy and I reached an understanding after we had a long talk in the barn the other day." Laughing, he asked, "Now, where is church being held today?"

"Oh, did I forget to tell you?" Abram

asked, shrugging. "We're going to the Bawell place. They have a large backyard."

Josie tugged at her *kapp* and stared straight ahead. Katy sat down beside her and straightened her deep blue dress. "You look pretty, Josie."

Josie glanced at her friend, wishing she had Katy's silky blond hair. "I feel drab next to you and all those curls."

Katy snorted. "I hate these curls, but we are not to be vain about that."

"I don't have a vain bone in my body," Josie admitted. "But I do have drab hair."

"Right now, with the sun coming through those big doors," Katy said, motioning toward the back of the benches lined up underneath the shade of several mushrooming oaks, "the sun makes your hair look like dark gold. You need to know that you are beautiful in God's eyes."

Josie smiled at her friend and then looked back since she loved seeing the sunshine shooting across the worship area. A group of men walked up and headed for the benches lining the other side, where the men sat separately from the women.

"Tobias," she said, before she could take it back.

Katy's blue eyes went wide. She turned to stare behind them. "The one you mentioned after you saw him in town?"

Josie managed to nod, but she felt dizzy, her heart racing.

"I should leave."

Katy's hand on hers stopped her. "That would only make things worse." Giving Josie a soft smile, she said, "I understand you don't want to be around him, but if you run out of here, everyone will notice. People will talk, Josie."

Josie huddled against her friend, tears pricking her eyes. "About me? About Tobias?"

She'd told Katy the whole truth on the buggy ride home—that she and Tobias had been engaged, but she'd left after another man had ruined her.

Katy had looked shocked at first, and then she'd nodded and hugged Josie close.

"No wonder you got so upset when you saw him. I will keep your secret, Josie. But you'll have to deal with him being here."

Now her friend gave her a questioning stare. "They might get the wrong impression," Katy said, her eyes filling with a meaningful warning. "That he might be the one."

"The baby's…" She stopped and put a hand to her mouth. "I never thought about that. I told you the other day—he is not. That's why I can't be around him. What should I do?"

Katy still held her hand. "You do what you need to do. You smile and stay kind. Being kind to a man you once loved is not a crime. In fact, it is the best thing you can do right now."

"And why is that?"

"If you treat him like you do all the other men who've tried to court you, he'll soon get the same message as they did."

Josie winced at that accurate description. "You have a good point."

"I always do," Katy said, her pert nose in the air. "Now take a deep breath and try to listen to the service."

Josie inhaled, taking in the scents of fresh air and clean clothes, the spring air flowing over the long rows of benches cool on her warm cheeks. She took in whiffs of pot roast and baked rolls, familiar smells that came with eating dinner after church. "You're right. If I act out, everyone will notice. I don't want anyone to think badly of Tobias."

Katy sighed and gave her a knowing smile. "Because you still care about him, don't you?"

Josie couldn't answer that question. But her friend bobbed her head. "That's what I thought."

"How are you?"

Josie whirled from clearing the table where she'd sat with some of the other women during dinner.

Tobias stood with a small bench balanced against his leg.

"I am fine," she responded, glad Rae-sha had taken the *kinder* inside to wash up. She did not want Tobias to see Dinah.

"You look better today," he said as he held the bench straight up next to him and watched her rake scraps off the table.

Josie tried to catch her breath. "Did I look that awful the other day?"

His gaze moved over her, warming her and chilling her at the same time. "You've always looked beautiful to me, Josie, but you were distraught and, honestly, you didn't make sense. You know you can talk to me, right?"

Josie stopped what she was doing and remembered none of this was his fault. "Did you send me flowers?"

"If I say yes, will you be angry?"

She studied him, taking her time to see him as a grown man now with broad, strong shoulders and a chiseled look that showed he was used to manual labor and hard work. "*Neh*, I would not be angry. But if you did send them, you should not do that again."

"Isn't sending flowers a part of the courting ritual?"

Josie's stomach tightened, memories cutting through her. "We are not courting. I shouldn't be talking to you, Tobias."

"Your brother told me it would be all right to say hello."

"My brother needs to mind his own business."

Tobias looked confused, but he didn't leave. Instead, he glanced around the rolling acreage and then back at the house where several buggies were still parked while their owners went to tend to their horses and harness them to leave. "This is a nice place. I hope you're happy here."

"I am."

She was as content as she could be, considering. Josie steeled herself against needing him, but having him so close made him hard to resist. So she focused on the sweet wind of late spring and tried to take soothing breaths.

"I understand you don't want me to buy your old home, but I don't understand why."

"It would be difficult, Tobias."

"Why? You're here, and now I'm here. I found you and I'd like us to get to know each other again."

"I already know you," she said, remembering their time together, her heart pierced with the sweet memories. Before she could stop herself, she added, "I could never forget you."

"I can never forget you, either," he said, his eyes bright with hope. "That is why I came to find you."

Josie felt panic rising in her stomach. "You shouldn't have come here. I told you, we cannot be together."

He stepped closer. "Josie, if you could just tell me what happened. What went wrong?"

"Josie?"

She pivoted to see Katy waving to her. Inhaling to find her next breath, she said, "I have to go inside and help with the dishes. *Denke* for the flowers. They are very pretty."

Then she turned and hurried into the

Bawell house as fast as she could. When she reached Katy, she grabbed her friend's arm. "*Denke*. I was so afraid I'd say the wrong thing."

Katy shifted and slanted her head to one side while she stared at Tobias and then looked back to give Josie a sympathetic glance. "I don't think you could say anything that would make that man go away, Josie. The way he looks at you is the way we all want a man to look at us—with love and longing, and respect."

"I do not deserve any of those things. And he deserves better."

Katy looped her arm in Josie's as they headed inside the house. "I do not agree with that. You could be doing a great dishonor to a man who is trying to show you he wants to make amends."

"He didn't do anything wrong," Josie replied, her tone sounding defensive. She would defend Tobias even while she refused to hope for any future with him.

Katy had other ideas. "Then you need to tell him that."

Josie heard her friend's suggestion. "Why does everyone seem to want to push Tobias and me together?"

Katy gave her another quiet stare. "Because maybe you two should be together?"

Josie considered that and everything else that held her and Tobias apart. What would he do if he found out her secret?

What if he went away forever?

She didn't think she could bear watching him walk away.

But he'd had to bear her doing that very thing.

"You're right," she told Katy after they'd tidied up the big kitchen while Raesha and some of the others went out for a stroll with the *kinder*. "I should at least apologize to Tobias for what I did."

"Is he still here?" Katy asked, looking outside.

"I don't know," Josie said. "But I will go and look for him."

She dried her hands on a white towel, straightened her clothing and pushed at her hair. Right now, this very moment, she wanted nothing more than to be near Tobias again.

Just to be near him.

Maybe they would both have to accept that as the only way they could coexist in the same community. But would Tobias accept that as the final solution?

Or would he give up on her and finally leave?

Josie walked out to the barn and searched the area. All of the church benches had been loaded up and put in a storage room here, or taken back to various homes around the community where they'd be stored in other barns.

When she didn't see Tobias anywhere, her heart sank. Maybe it was for the best that she didn't try to talk to him anyway. Would he accept her apology without her having to tell him anything more?

Then she turned back to the house and saw Tobias standing with Abram Schrock and her brother. They were talking low and looked serious.

What were they discussing?

* * *

Tobias listened as Josiah explained how the hat shop worked. Raesha ran the shop and took care of her home, while Josiah worked the land and tended the milking and the livestock. Josiah had some knowledge of growing cash crops, so Tobias had been asking for his advice. Abram had joined them.

"So you not only have a talent with wood, but you want to grow farm-fresh crops for fancy restaurants?" Abram asked, shaking his head. "This young one is a hard worker, Josiah. If you sell him that place of yours, I am thinking you two could team up and have a nice setup here."

Josiah gave Tobias a sharp glance. "That all depends, Abram. I haven't decided if I'm ready to sell or not."

Abram looked confused. "I see. Well, I hope you make up your mind soon enough. I don't want to see Tobias leave. He has a true talent and he brags on my wife's cooking, both of which make my life a lot easier."

Josiah shot Tobias another glance as he smiled at Abram's wit. "I am glad to hear that, Abram."

Tobias was about to change the subject when he looked up and saw Josie watching him. "Excuse me," he said, not caring what anyone thought. He walked over to where she stood by the breezeway between the two houses.

"Josie? What is wrong?"

Josie held on to her apron, her fingers twisting the heavy cotton. "I need to say something to you."

His heart lifted like the wings of a dove. "Okay."

"I'm sorry, Tobias. Sorry that I left you when we had such plans for the future. I know I hurt you. I need you to forgive me."

Confused, he looked into her eyes and saw the regret there. "I do forgive you. I would not be here if I wasn't able to do that. But I need answers, Josie."

She lowered her gaze, then lifted her chin, her eyes meeting his. "I cannot give you answers, Tobias. We can be friends but nothing more. You must accept that."

He shook his head. "I *cannot* accept that. I can forgive, but it is hard to think that you don't love me anymore."

"I didn't say that," she blurted, tears in her eyes.

He took a small step and stopped, but his eyes brightened. "So you might still have feelings for me?"

"No." She twisted the apron corners against her clenched fists, her knuckles white. "I feel friendship for you and I have our memories, but nothing beyond that. I want you to know I'm sorry."

Frustration filled his heart. "I'm trying, Josie. But it's hard to see you and not be able to understand."

He turned to leave but Raesha came out, a little girl holding her hand. He looked at her and then back at Josie.

Josie went pale, her eyes moving over the little girl.

"JoJo," the child said, running to her.

Raesha hurried to the child. "Dinah, your aunt JoJo is busy right now. *Kumm*."

"JoJo," Dinah said, giggling as she held up her hand for Josie to take, her smile shining with love.

Josie's tormented gaze moved from Raesha back to Tobias.

Then she lifted Dinah in her arms. "I need to tend to Raesha's daughter, Tobias. It was nice to talk to you."

She took the little girl back into the house, leaving Tobias standing there staring behind her.

"Give her time," Raesha said. "She has come a long way to get back home, Tobias."

"*Ja*, and I have come a long way to find her," he replied. Then he turned to leave, knowing in his heart they were all keeping something from him.

He had a feeling the "something" might involve that beautiful little girl. The little girl who had such a familiar face, but a face he couldn't bring to his memory. Maybe the child just reminded him of Josie. There was a striking resemblance.

Dejected, he turned and walked back toward where Abram now stood at their buggy, Beth waiting inside.

"Is everything all right, Tobias?" Abram asked, his voice drenched with concern.

"*Ja*, just meeting some of Josiah's family."

Abram nodded. "Josie is available, you know."

Tobias shook his head. "Not from what I can tell," he replied. Then he hopped up on the buggy and started back toward the Schrock home.

He wished with all of his heart he could make Josie see reason, so they could have their own home. Just as they'd planned so long ago.

Chapter Nine

Josie clipped back the mint, weeding the tiny herb garden, the scents of lavender and basil wafting through the air. A storm had passed through the night and left the garden green and freshly washed. She loved tending to this little herb crop since it was close to the house and out of sight from the tourists who came to the hat shop in droves during the high season.

Why were the *Englisch* so fascinated with the plain life, when they carried fancy purses and backpacks and always had their noses glued to their cell phones? She had an inkling of life outside this peaceful valley, and at first she'd enjoyed the freedom of making her own decisions. But being alone and pregnant soon changed her mind. There was a certain peace in knowing your boundaries and abiding by God's grace and law.

She never wanted to stray back into that world, and since she'd confessed and been baptized, she'd be shunned if she ever left again.

But now she had one more reason to stay.

Tobias.

He truly was trying to court her. Since the Sunday they'd talked right here near the house, he'd sent her a drawing of a horse that looked similar to the miniature he'd carved for her out of black oak wood. The little horse sat on a dresser in her bedroom. Naomi had asked her about it once, when she'd found Josie holding the horse in her hand.

"A friend back in Kentucky carved this for me," she'd told Naomi. "I cannot give it away."

"You don't need to give it away," Naomi had replied. "We all have little treasures we cherish."

Then Naomi had shown Josie a beautiful brooch her late husband had given her one Christmas. "He told me an *Englisch* man had given it to him after he'd helped him plant his garden. His wife had died and he wanted someone else to enjoy it."

The brooch had been small and crusted with pearls. Josie understood why Naomi never wore it. Jewelry did not fit the plain ways. "It's a treasure for you?"

"Yes, because my husband made another person happy by giving it to me. Just as that little bonnet you placed on Dinah's head when you left her on our doorstep was a treasure to you. Treasures hold memories, so you hold tight to your little horse. Just remember *Gott* has given us the greatest treasure. He has given us His love and our Christ."

Josie sat back now and pushed at her hair, the basket of mint next to her filling her senses with its sweetness. She closed her eyes and imagined what her life might have been like if she could have stayed in Kentucky and married Tobias.

"Josie?"

She opened her eyes and saw him coming toward her. Josie couldn't move, couldn't speak. Was she dreaming?

"Josie, Raesha told me you were back here."

Why did everyone try to mess in her life?

Her heart rushing too fast, she said, "I don't need any company."

Tobias came closer, his dark hair curling around his ears. "She also told me you'd say that."

Josie tried to rise up off the low porch and almost toppled back. Tobias dropped the bag he'd been carrying. He was there to catch her, his strong hands on her arms sending shock waves throughout her system.

After he righted her, he held to her arms. "I brought you something."

Josie couldn't breathe. He was so close,

she could reach out and touch his face, sink her fingers into his hair, hold him close. "What did you bring?"

He let her go, his gaze warm on her face. Then he reached down and picked up the bag. "Beth Schrock made some fried pies and sent them with Abram this morning. He gave me several, and I remembered how you love a good fried pie—especially peach."

He pulled a wrapped pie out of the bag. "I have apple, too. Beth is a great cook."

Josie took the offering, wondering what she should do. Tobias had always been a thoughtful man, but he remembered things she'd tried to forget. *"Denke."*

He stood watching her. "Aren't you going to eat it?"

Josie's heart opened a little tiny bit. *"Ja.* I'm terribly hungry." She motioned to the porch steps. "Why don't you join me?"

Tobias bobbed his head. "I am on a break, so I cannot stay long. But I've been hankering for the apple one all morning."

Josie took little bites of the sweet folded

dough that enclosed the juicy peaches. "Beth must have some leftover preserves since our peaches will not be ripe until July."

"I believe so," Tobias replied, his smile so beautiful it brought tears to her eyes. "I didn't ask. I just wanted to taste these. With you."

Josie smiled, the feel of smiling at Tobias foreign and unfamiliar but easy at this moment. "It was kind of you to think of me. You came all the way from town?"

He looked sheepish, his cheeks reddening and his eyes downcast. "I had a delivery nearby and I planned to eat all of these on the way. But... I thought of you, so I am willing to share."

They sat in silence, munching away on the flaky crust and the sweet, syrupy fruit inside. Josie glanced over at her old home. "My *mamm* used to make these."

Tobias stopped eating, glanced at the house and then back at her. "Do you want to talk about your *mamm*?"

Josie turned to him, fear clutching at her

throat. Quickly wrapping the rest of her fried pie back into the cloth that had covered it, she stood. "*Neh.* I... I have to go inside and take care of these herbs."

Then she grabbed her basket and hurried up the steps. But she turned at the door. "I enjoyed sitting with you, Tobias."

After hurrying inside, she slammed the door and leaned against it, the rich pie she'd eaten settling like a splintered log inside her roiling stomach.

She could not let this happen. She wouldn't do this again.

Because the more Tobias came around, the more she'd want to be with him. And she could never be with him. She knew that, and if she told him the truth, then he'd know that, too.

Maybe it was time she did just that. Tell him the truth—the one thing that would make him leave Campton Creek for good.

A week later, Josie still hadn't found the courage to approach Tobias. She'd managed to avoid him since seeing him at church, yet she had to wonder what he'd thought about Dinah. Had he recognized his former friend's resemblance in her face and eyes? Or did he only see that she looked a lot like Josie?

Living like this was torment, but she had work to do today. She also now had a plan that would test her strength as much as seeing Tobias again had.

"So you want to go to the Spring Festival tomorrow?"

Josie nodded, her hands held together over her apron, hoping Katy wouldn't question her too much. "*Ja.* I need to get out more, and now that summer is coming, I feel better about being around people my own age. I did promise Raesha I'd help in the Bawell booth. We'll be selling quilts and hats along with our jams and baked goods, of course." Then she lifted her hand. "Not to mention the goat-milk soaps and lotions. They are favorites with the *Englisch.*"

"It's good for you to get out and help," Katy said. "Do you hope to see Tobias there?" Katy held one hand on her hip and her lips twisted to hide her smile.

"Tobias might not attend. He's not a part of this community."

Katy frowned at that. "But Abram and Beth have been including him in everything that goes on around here. Trying to find him a perfect match, I believe." She added, "Surely, he'll help Abram with the furniture booth."

Josie's stomach dropped at that innocently spoken notion. Or from the smug look in her friend's eyes, maybe not so innocently. "He needs to get to know people, so it makes sense they'd try to introduce him to others who are young and...single."

"He is young and he is single," Katy replied. "But he only searches for you in the crowds."

"I'm going to get out of the house and make more friends," Josie retorted. "Because the friend standing beside me now can be annoying at times."

Katy playfully took her arm. "I do not

care why you've decided to go, but I'm glad you're going. I'll be busy looking for Samson Miller, so you will be on your own part of the time."

Katy had a crush on Samson and Josie was her only confidante regarding that. Samson didn't have a clue. Or pretended not to have a clue.

"I'll be busy working at our booth." Josie moved around the hat shop, packing the bonnets and men's summer straw hats they'd take to the annual festival. They made all sorts of hats, many of them fitted to size and to the district's specifications. They also made some fancier hats and bonnets that appealed to the *Englisch*. "Did you come here to help me pack things or to tease me?"

"I am marking the bags and boxes as you requested," Katy said, holding up a marker as proof.

Josie thought about being around other young adults, girls and boys becoming women and men who were looking for someone to marry and start a life with.

Then finding homes and planting gardens, growing a family and making plans. The festival would be full of Amish families, and most of the folks her age would migrate to the food booths and find quiet places to get to know each other.

How she longed for that kind of life, but she feared she'd be single and alone forever, especially if something ever happened to Naomi. So she'd decided the best thing she could do was find someone to marry. Anyone. Anyone but the man she longed to be with. She wanted to tell him the truth, but each time she envisioned that, it brought her only pain and shame.

If Tobias heard she'd moved on, maybe he would, too. She hadn't decided how to handle telling another man her horrible secret, but she'd worry about that once Tobias was gone. If she got a marriage proposal, she could call off the wedding once Tobias had left. Because she'd rather be alone than marry someone she didn't love. She'd either leave or stay away from everyone so no one would bother her again.

Katy had a point. What if Tobias showed up this afternoon?

He had been seen around town a lot by many people, single women who would like to get to know him better. He was young and strong, and he made furniture that would last a lifetime. She hadn't thought about him being at the festival.

That made her heart pierce with an agonizing pain that cut her breath away. She adjusted her shoulders and breathed in. She had to pretend she didn't care.

"I don't mind being on my own," she replied to Katy's earlier warning. "I have learned to accept that." Then she added, "I need to find someone to court me."

Katy gave her a hard stare, her grimace almost comical. "Courting? You're going courting? Is this what you truly want, or is this plan to scare off Tobias?"

"Both."

Katy shook her head and gave Josie a quick hug. "I hope Tobias is there and I hope you will talk to *him*. Talking never hurt anyone, but using another man to avoid Tobias is wrong. It's unkind."

Katy was smart and wise, but words could hurt and Josie knew that better than others. How could she deceive a man who'd done nothing wrong? "I will be kind if I see Tobias," she said. "Being kind does not hurt anyone, either."

"That is so true." Katy grinned. "I'm glad you are going."

Josie wasn't glad, but she would put on a good front. She'd learned a lot about deception over the last few years. She prayed every night for forgiveness, but she was caught up in a web that only stretched and grew with each day. The weight of that delicate web tugged at her shoulders like a yoke.

That yoke would grow even heavier when she deceived everyone yet again. But what other choice did she have?

Chapter Ten

Tobias inhaled a deep breath. The day was full of sunshine and the scents of good food cooking over grills and fires. Chicken and roast beef for sandwiches, casseroles and cakes to take home for dinner, cookies and other sweets to sell to both Amish and *Englisch* alike. Tobias had *Englisch* friends back in Kentucky who liked to sample Amish food and sometimes help with the hard work around the farm. He'd partied with some of them during his *rumspringa*. But he got over that pretty quickly when he realized they could get rowdy at times.

After he met Josie, he took her to a few *Englisch* get-togethers. But she didn't seem to enjoy them much. She liked staying close to home, with chaperones nearby. Still, Tobias had managed to sweet-talk her into attending some of the big parties his *Englisch* friends liked to throw.

Campton Creek wasn't any more isolated than the Kentucky community he'd left, but it was much bigger and more spread out. Tobias had to admit this community had a lot going on. Cars and buggies stretched as far as he could see in the clear field just outside of town where the festivals and mud sales apparently were held several months out of each year. He marveled at the many colorful booths that held so many commodities. Maybe next year he'd set up his own booth selling fresh produce like several others along the way.

"What do you think of our little festival?" Abram asked as he handed Tobias a footstool they'd created out of thick grapevines a driftwood gatherer had sold to Abram.

The legs and feet were twisted but sturdy and varnished a deep brown, the oval stool bottom covered with a padded navy twill cushion surrounded by small twisted and varnished vines. It would make someone happy to have this little stool to rest their tired feet upon.

"I am impressed," Tobias admitted. "This is a lot bigger than the mud sales and bazaars we had back in Kentucky."

He'd sold a lot of fresh vegetables at the farmers' market in Orchard Mountain. That had given him the idea of the farm-to-table "side hustle," as his *Englisch* friends had called it.

"I could get used to this," he admitted to Abram.

"We aim to please," Abram retorted with a wry grin. "I'm extremely pleased with the extra pieces you made, Tobias. Those little wooden toys will be a hit."

Tobias beamed with pride as he set out the horses, dogs, baby goats and kittens he'd carved in several sizes, sometimes late at night when he couldn't sleep. He carved when he was worried or nervous, and he'd surely been both of those things over the last few weeks. He'd also brought some from Kentucky, which he hoped to sell today.

Thinking of Josie, he searched the long alleyways to see if she'd arrived. The Bawell Hat Shop tent was a large one with rows and rows of straw hats with black bands around them, all made by hand with a team of experts. Something all Amish men would need for summer. He noticed prayer *kapps* in both black and white, aprons and women's heavier winter bonnets, too. Theirs was a true, thriving business that attracted a lot of people in both cars and buggies, from what he'd noticed in passing.

Would Josie be here to help inside the booth?

He hoped so. He had prayed to find a way to reach her, but he was losing hope each day. He hadn't sent her anything since the day he'd offered her a fruit pie. She'd ended their sweet time together there on the breezeway in an abrupt manner.

Questions he'd held long inside his soul resurfaced each time he was around her, but he refused to give up.

"Where's your head?" Abram asked, giving him a worried glance.

"Sorry, I was just lost in thought," Tobias admitted. "I want a home, Abram. And a wife and children."

"Well, I want those things for you, too," Abram replied, his hands on his hips. "Any word about the Fisher place?"

"No. Not yet. I have a few more weeks."

"A few more weeks for what?" Abram asked.

Realizing he'd slipped up, Tobias said, "To convince Josiah I'll take *gut* care of the place."

"Oh, that. He'll see that in your actions and your attitude. And meantime, I think my Beth is seriously working on finding you the perfect wife."

Tobias already knew who would be the

perfect wife. He would have to tell Abram and Beth the truth, but not today. They had too much to do today, and he didn't want to mar their plans to sell lots of furniture. He'd explain everything to them next time they sat down to a meal together at home.

Home.

Campton Creek was beginning to feel that way.

He looked up and saw Josie walking toward the Bawell booth, her back to him. She carried a woven basket and wore a blue dress and a white *kapp* and apron, but he could find her slim form no matter how many people or things separated them.

No matter how much she refused to admit that she still cared about him. Tobias would find a way, somehow, to make her see that they still belonged together. No matter what.

Maybe he should tell her that so she'd see that, together and with *Gott*'s guidance, they could get through anything.

* * *

"Have you seen him yet?"

Josie nodded at Katy's impatient question. "*Ja*, so stop asking me that."

They were sitting behind the Bawell tent, eating a lunch of chicken-salad sandwiches and sliced apples. Josie had grabbed two oatmeal cookies for their dessert.

"Well?" Katy's blue eyes got even bigger. "I would like details."

"There are no details," Josie said. "He's still a very handsome man."

"You should go and visit with him."

"You should mind your own business. Where is Samson Miller, by the way?"

Katy threw a potato chip at her. "He is in his family's booth, selling fresh eggs and goat cheese."

"Sounds exciting."

Katy giggled. "Samson is a single-minded person. He can't be bothered to eat lunch when he's got eggs to sell."

Josie glanced up and thought about how earlier she'd spotted Tobias in the Schrock booth. She didn't dare venture over to that side of the alley, but she could make out his form as he lifted a chair off a parked wagon, his arms strong and sure, his hair always curling underneath his hat. He had the bluest eyes, so like the sky today. His smile had always made her feel special, but now that smile only brought her pain and regret.

Glad they had been busy, she tried not to think of him walking on the same soil as her. Tried not to notice the bevy of young Amish women who seemed to suddenly have a keen interest in furniture and wood carvings.

When she saw Mary Zook walking by with a carved kitten, she knew instantly Tobias had created the work. Her gasp caught Katy's attention.

Katy made an eye roll. "Mary, such a flirt. I guess she had a long discussion with Tobias about wood shavings."

Josie spun to look back at the furniture tent. She didn't see Tobias there. "Maybe he's left already."

"Or maybe he's searching for Mary, Mary, quite ready to marry."

"Stop it," Josie retorted, her words sharp.

"Just as I thought," Katy said. "You are jealous."

Josie dropped her half-eaten cookie. "I am not jealous. I want Tobias to be happy."

"Without you?"

"He cannot be with me."

"He could if you'd just talk to him."

Josie had talked to him, and each time only made things more painful. "He understands."

"Really?" Katy looked beyond her. "Maybe you can ask him if he truly understands, because he's coming toward our booth right now."

Josie stood and went back inside the booth. She saw Tobias walking the alley-way between the merchants, people all around him, his gaze on the Bawell booth.

Mary Zook walked back by and waved to Tobias, her dimples shining. He nodded, his gaze straight ahead. Mary looked discouraged and kept walking.

"I'm taking a stroll," Katy said before she darted away. Raesha had gone to their buggy to feed Daniel, and Dinah was home with Naomi and a neighbor who was watching them both.

Josie was alone in the booth.

Tobias walked right up to where she stood and leaned over the small wooden counter Josiah and some others had set up earlier. "Good afternoon," he said, his smile soft and reassuring.

"Hello." She didn't know what to say, so she sat back on the tall stool and stared at him. "Are you enjoying the festival?"

"Very much." He didn't take his eyes away from her. "A lot of people around."

"Is Abram pleased? Are you selling a lot?"

"We've been steady busy, *ja*."

Josie was running out of small talk. "*Denke* again for the peach pie. I enjoyed it." Glancing at the people milling about, she asked, "Shouldn't you get back?"

"I'm on break," he replied, his eyes full of that mischief she remembered so well. "I wanted to spend it with my best girl."

Josie's throat caught. He'd always called her that. "I'm not that girl anymore, Tobias."

"Josie," he said, his eyes serious now, "whatever happened, whatever you're afraid of, I will handle it—for both of us. I will carry your burdens."

Tears burned but she held tightly to her control. "It is my burden only, Tobias."

Before she knew what was happening, Tobias came around, slipped inside the booth and sat down on the stool beside her without saying a word.

"You shouldn't," she said, her voice shaky now. "You need to go."

"I'm going in a few minutes," he said. He took her hand in his, careful that no one would notice. "I made you something."

He slipped the warm piece of wood into her palm and held it there between their laced fingers. "I will carry your burdens, Josie."

Josie couldn't speak, couldn't move. What if Raesha or Josiah came back? What if she had a customer?

But the world around her seemed to recede as Tobias held her hand in his, the carving warm between them, the world away from them. The touch of his skin ricocheted through her system like a ray of warm sunshine, bringing a peace she hadn't felt in years. She lifted her hand away and saw the delicate butterfly he'd shaped out of what looked like an exotic wood.

"Tobias," she whispered, ready to pour out her heart.

Tobias stood, his expression full of love and understanding. And hope.

"Excuse me."

They both looked up to find an *Englisch* man standing there, his world-weary gaze reading them with a sharp clarity.

Josie stood up, the small carving still in her hand. She recognized Nathan Craig, the private investigator who helped the Amish with missing people or legal problems. He'd helped her brother find her. "Nathan, it is *gut* to see you."

"Nice to see you, Josie," Nathan said. Then he turned to Tobias and introduced himself, giving Tobias a handshake. "Actually, Mr. Mast, I've been looking for you. I didn't want to do this here, but it's a timely matter and I had to locate you today."

Tobias looked surprised. "Me? Why?"

Josie didn't know what to say. Why was a private investigator looking for Tobias?

"Maybe we should speak in private," Nathan suggested, his tone determined.

Tobias glanced at Josie. "I don't mind Josie hearing. I trust her."

Josie felt the volt of appreciation from that comment, only to be followed by a sharp pang of regret. "I cannot leave the booth anyway. What's going on, Nathan?"

Nathan said, "I got a call from an associate in Kentucky. He says an English couple is trying to track Tobias down because you were once friends with their son."

Tobias looked perplexed. "*Ja*, I knew a lot of *Englisch* during my *rumspringa*. Who is this couple?"

"Theodore and Pamela Benington," Nathan said, his shrewd gaze sweeping over both of them. "They have a son named Drew. Do you remember him?"

Josie grabbed the stool and sank down on it, her heart on fire, her pulse pounding like a hammer to nails.

Drew Benington?

Tobias glanced at Josie, concern in his eyes. "I did know him. But I heard he got into some trouble and is now in prison."

"He is," Nathan said. "They only want to ask you some questions and I'm not at liberty to say what they are looking for. My associate only asked me to alert you so you can plan accordingly. The Beningtons are flying up here and they should arrive late tomorrow afternoon. They'd like to meet with you at the Campton Center on Monday if possible."

Tobias nodded. "I have no idea why they'd want to see me," he said. "I haven't talked to Drew in years."

Nathan shot Josie a look that could have been a warning. "As I said, I don't have the details, but can you be there around two o'clock?"

Tobias nodded. "I'll be there. I have to get back to my booth now." He turned to Josie. "We will talk later."

She couldn't speak. She only nodded, the wooden butterfly carving clutched in her hand.

After Tobias hurried back to the furniture booth, Nathan looked at Josie. "Are you okay?"

She shot up off the stool, her hands holding on to the counter with a painful grip. "You know everything, don't you?"

Nathan rubbed a hand over his chin. "I know enough, but I had to find Tobias and give him the message. Josie, do you also know Drew Benington?"

She moved her head, tears pricking at her eyes. "I did."

Nathan didn't ask any more questions. He only nodded. "Josie, if Drew was your attacker and Tobias doesn't know the truth, you need to tell him. The Beningtons are here to make amends for what their son has done. I can't be sure what they already know and it's not my place to ask. But Tobias needs to hear the truth from you before they tell him. If you need me or Alisha, let us know, all right?"

"Why would I need a lawyer?" she asked, knowing his wife did legal work for the Amish.

"You might not, but if their son told them what he did to you, they might want some answers and they might ask to see you, too. I couldn't tell you that in front of Tobias, since I wasn't sure. Always a good idea to have counsel in the room since this is a delicate and difficult situation."

Josie gasped and put her hand to her mouth. "I went to them early on and tried to tell them, but they refused to listen to me. They didn't believe me when I told them I was pregnant, but, Nathan, I tried to explain. They told me to go away."

Nathan glanced around to make sure they were alone. "If they've somehow verified your pregnancy, the Beningtons might be coming here to talk to you, too. Just be aware. They'll want to speak to you if they have all the facts and they'll want definitive proof."

Josie's stomach roiled. "You mean about Dinah. You don't think they'd try to take her?"

Nathan's expression turned grim. "I don't know and I shouldn't be speculating with you. But they're coming, regardless of why. Even though Alisha helped Josiah and Raesha with all the legalities of the adoption, you still need to warn your family."

Alisha Braxton, the lawyer who'd guided them through making sure Dinah could stay with Josiah while Josie was still missing. And now Nathan's wife. She'd assured them everything had been by the book. What if she'd missed something?

Nathan looked her over. "Do you want me to call someone for you?"

"Neh." She straightened some crocheted doilies. "Raesha would worry. I'll explain all of this to them when we get home, not here."

"I'm sorry I had to be the one to alert you, but Tobias was here with you, so I didn't know how to handle it. Let me know if you need anything."

She nodded again, grateful that Nathan and Alisha had helped Josiah find her and figure out what had happened to her and Dinah. Along with Judy Campton, they had helped her family in many ways. Nathan had no choice but to tell his associate the truth—that Tobias was here now.

She only wished Nathan had warned her earlier, but he'd found her and Tobias together and had to move fast. Why did Drew's parents want to see Tobias? Would they try to turn Tobias against her? Or would they try to take Dinah away?

She couldn't let that happen. It would

destroy her whole family. They all loved Dinah.

Nathan wouldn't repeat anything to anyone not involved. But her friend Sarah back in Kentucky knew everything. Had Sarah been forced to tell Drew's parents the truth? Or did they remember how, in a fit of desperation, Josie had blurted out the facts? Facts they'd refused to believe.

Raesha came back to the booth, smiling down at little Daniel as he bounced in her arms. "Was that Nathan Craig?" she asked, her keen gaze sweeping over Josie and then back to the departing man.

Josie nodded while Raesha settled the babe inside his portable crib. "He was just passing by."

She'd have to tell her family about this, but right now she felt a panic attack about to overtake her.

Her world, which just moments ago had seemed to right itself when Tobias was holding her hand, had come crumbling down once again.

The parents of the boy who'd assaulted

her would soon be in Campton Creek.
And they needed to talk to Tobias.

She had no choice but to tell him the
truth. But when and how could she do that?

Chapter Eleven

The hours seemed to drag as heavily as the weight on her shoulders. Josie watched the Schrock booth and saw Tobias talking to customers and helping people load furniture. He had to be wondering what was going on.

Josie tried to engage with customers and friends, but finally she told Raesha she wasn't feeling well. Tobias had left the furniture booth and she had no idea where he'd gone.

"Do you want to go home?" Raesha asked, concern in her eyes. "I can get someone from one of the other booths or from the youth group to help."

Josie nodded. "I can walk home. That might do me good."

Raesha smiled at some lookers and then turned back to Josie. "Are you sure? You look pale."

Josie pushed at her sleeves. "I think it's all the people. I thought I could do this, but I'm sorry, Raesha. I just need to be alone and I don't mind walking."

Raesha smiled as she handed a bag of bread and homemade strawberry jam to an Amish woman and took the payment. Then she pivoted around to face Josie. "A walk might do you good. Just be careful."

"I'll be fine. The road is very open. I'll take the shortcut."

Josie glanced down the way at the furniture booth. She hadn't seen Tobias since he'd left an hour ago. Maybe she'd get word to him before he talked to the Beningtons.

"I'm going to tell Katy I'm leaving," she

said, giving Daniel a kiss and nodding to Raesha.

Making her way along the alley filled with people, she went to the Schrock Furniture booth. Abram saw her and waved.

"Hi," she said, glancing around. "I was looking for Tobias."

Abram gave her a knowing smile. "He went to lunch and then he had a delivery to make. I doubt he'll be back until time to load up and clear out."

Disappointment warred with relief in Josie's head. She had to do this, but maybe she could find Tobias along the route home. "I'll talk to him later, then. *Denke.*"

Abram smiled. "Tobias is a good man, Josie. I hope you find him."

Like so many, Abram wanted her and Tobias to be together. That could never happen, especially now when her whole world was falling apart.

She left the big field and followed the path past all the cars and buggies, trying to stay away from anyone who might stop and talk with her. After looking everywhere, she didn't find Tobias at any of the lunch booths. Maybe he'd gone on home to the Schrock place after his delivery. That was too far in the other direction to get to and back before dark, and people would notice if she went there alone.

She'd send word somehow to let him know she needed to see him. She just hoped she wouldn't be too late.

Monday morning, Tobias explained to Bettye and Jewel that he was to meet the Beningtons at Campton Center at two o'clock. "I'm sorry for the short notice but they were firm on the day and time."

With no church yesterday, he'd managed to stay busy in the barn while Abram and Beth went visiting. But he'd thought about going to see Josie. Her reaction to hearing about Drew had puzzled him.

"We live for short notice," Jewel said, bringing him out of his worries. "I'll pull out some cookies and brew a big pot of coffee. Sounds like you've got some business to tend to."

"I have no idea what they want," Tobias replied, worry scorching his insides. "I did hear Drew went to prison, but I'm not sure why."

"Maybe he's getting out and he wants to make amends," Bettye suggested, her gaze meeting Jewel's.

"Could be," Jewel replied.

Tobias figured they knew something but weren't talking. He'd just have to wait and see. He couldn't stop thinking of how Josie had sunk down on her stool, shock draining the color from her face. She'd never liked Drew and had stopped going to the *Englisch* house parties a few weeks before she'd left. Was she upset that he might still be Drew's friend?

He'd have to explain that he hadn't seen Drew in a long time. Tobias had been so distraught after Josie disappeared, he didn't go to many social gatherings, *Englisch* or Amish. Then he had to take care of his *daed*, which meant he barely left the farm unless it was to take Daed to doctor appointments and to pick up supplies. Curiosity was making him antsy and on edge.

As the time to meet drew near, he left work and walked back over to the Campton Center. Jewel met him in the hallway and then placed a thermal coffeepot and water on the big table where the pro bono counselors and lawyers met with people. When they heard a knock at the door, Jewel hurried to open it.

Tobias sat, white-knuckled and worried, Bettye with him.

"I'm praying," Bettye said. "No matter what, Tobias, we're here when you need us."

Jewel walked back in, followed by Nathan Craig with a woman dressed in a dark suit and an older man and woman.

Jewel said, "Tobias, you've met Nathan. This is his wife, Alisha, who is a lawyer. And this is Mr. and Mrs. Theodore Benington."

Tobias stood and nodded. "Hello." Why had they brought a lawyer?

The woman with golden-brown shoulder-length hair answered his unasked question, her tone all business. "I'm here as a mediator, nothing more."

Now he needed a mediator?

Jewel and Bettye discreetly left, shutting the door behind them.

Tobias sat back down after everyone had found a place. "What is this about?"

The older woman's eyes teared up. "I'm Pamela, Drew's mother. We're here because he asked us to find you."

"He wants you to forgive him," Mr. Benington said, his voice shaky.

"Forgive him?" Tobias shook his head. "For what?"

The older couple looked at Alisha. She nodded.

Pamela leaned across the table. "He's ill, Tobias. Liver cancer. He's in prison, but he's dying, so he insisted we come here to find you. He needs forgiveness."

Tobias lowered his head. "I am sorry to hear of this, but Drew owes me nothing. We were friends for a season and then we went our separate ways. You didn't need to come all this way to tell me that."

Alisha cleared her throat. "Tobias, the Beningtons are here today because their son begged them to find you. But he wanted them to find another person, too."

"Who?" Tobias asked, more perplexed than ever.

"Josie Fisher," Alisha said, her gaze moving from him to her husband.

Josie's frantic worry had mounted by the hour. Yesterday she'd begged Katy to drive her to the Schrock place so she could talk to Tobias, but no one had answered the door. Worried that he'd found out the worst and left before she could explain, she'd told Josiah and Raesha about the Beningtons. She couldn't put it off any longer.

"I don't know what they want," she said after they'd all had the midday dinner. "But I have to find Tobias before they talk to him. I tried yesterday, but he was nowhere to be found. If they know about me, they'll tell him. And then they'll want to see Dinah."

Naomi's gaze held hers. "But how would they possibly know about Dinah?"

Josie wiped at her eyes. "I went to them one night when I became desperate and… told them I might be pregnant. They refused to believe me and told me to get out of their house. After that, I ran away."

"You never told us that," Raesha said.

"It didn't seem to matter," Josie admitted. "They did not believe me and their son wanted nothing to do with me. They only thought I was trying to trick their son into marriage, which I never wanted."

Raesha gasped and grabbed Josiah's arm. "They can't take her, can they? They won't take Dinah away?"

Josiah paled, reaching for his wife. "I do not know. They might not even realize a child is involved." He let go of Raesha and tugged Josie close. "We cannot say what they know or why they are here."

"We should call Alisha," Raesha said, wiping her eyes. "She can advise us same as she did when Dinah first arrived. She handled the adoption and told us we were clear to raise Dinah. We have all of the paperwork."

Naomi moved her wheelchair closer and reached for Raesha's hand. "Do not fret. Don't go borrowing worry."

Josie cried against her brother's fresh-smelling shirt. "I have to find Tobias. Now."

"I'll take you into town," Josiah said, nodding to Raesha and Naomi. "We'll find him and I'll be there, nearby, when you tell him."

Naomi nodded and held tightly to Raesha's hand. "We will pray while we wait for your return."

Now Josie sat in the buggy beside her brother, remembering when she'd first returned to Campton Creek. Back then, she had been numb and afraid and ashamed. Today she was stronger but still afraid. If Drew's parents took Dinah, her family would never get over losing their little girl.

She would never get over losing her own child.

"They have money, *bruder*. They can hire lawyers and make things hard for us."

Josiah hushed her. "We have love and we know a good lawyer. We did everything right, Josie. Alisha made sure of that."

When they reached town, Josie's nerves scattered and scurried. She couldn't breathe, couldn't think about what she'd say to Tobias.

"He should be at work," she told Josiah. "I'll go in and find him. We can go somewhere private to talk."

She hurried toward the store, her heart racing. Somehow she had to find the words and the courage to tell Tobias her secret. At long last.

Praying with all of her heart, Josie rushed into the market, the scents of cedar and pine only reminding her of Tobias.

"Well, where's the fire?" Abram asked from behind the counter. "Are you all right, Josie?"

"I need to talk to Tobias," she said, out of breath.

Abram's expression changed from jolly to dour. "He's not here. He had to meet with some people over at the Campton Center. Want me to give him a message?"

Shock caused Josie to go limp against the counter. "I'm too late."

Abram came around and sat her down on a chair. "What is wrong, Josie?"

"I need to tell him something important," she said, tears misting in her eyes.

Abram patted her shoulder. "Does it have to do with the people he's talking to? He told me about that."

She nodded, unable to speak.

"Then go and find him. You might be of some help to him."

Josie doubted that, but she didn't have a choice. Maybe she could get to him before the Beningtons did. "*Denke*, Abram."

She stood and steadied herself. "I have to go."

Abram watched her hurry away, but she didn't care anymore what anyone thought.

Except for Tobias. She wished now she'd told him the truth right away. But she'd been foolish and prideful. Thinking of the beautiful, delicate butterfly he'd carved for her, Josie found her strength.

She had to do the right thing. Tobias deserved that much at least.

Tobias stared at the couple across from him. "Did you say Josie?"

Pamela nodded. "Drew especially wanted us to find Josie. He's unable to come and tell her himself, but he wants her to know he's sorry."

Tobias leaned against the table. "Sorry for what?"

The front door burst open, causing all of them to glance toward the hallway. Tobias heard Jewel talking to someone and then footsteps approaching.

Jewel knocked on the partially open door. "I'm sorry to interrupt, but, Tobias, someone is here to see you."

"I can't... Can they wait?"

"No." Jewel's eyes went wide, her brows

lifting like two dark wings, while she tried to communicate with him. "It's urgent."

Still reeling from what they'd said to him about Josie, Tobias stood and glanced at Nathan and Alisha. "I'm sorry. I'll be right back."

They nodded and turned to continue talking to the Beningtons. Probably to keep them occupied until they could give Tobias more information.

Tobias hurried out into the hallway. "What is going on, Jewel?"

"She's out in the sunroom," Jewel said, giving him a gentle shove. "Go on now."

Tobias walked to the back of the house and stopped at the door to the sunroom.

Josie sat on a wicker chair with her head down and her hands twisted against her apron.

"Josie?" He hurried into the room and knelt in front of her. "What are you doing here?"

Josie lifted her head, tears streaming down her face. "I have to talk to you and tell you what happened. Before they do."

Tobias touched his hand to her tears. "You mean Drew's parents? They said Drew had a message for you." A sense of dread settled over him. "Drew did something to hurt you, didn't he?"

Her eyes filled with more tears, fear and dread darkening her gaze. "What...what was the message from Drew?"

Leaving his hand on her warm cheek, Tobias said, "He wanted you to know he's sorry." Then he dropped his hand and looked into her eyes. "Why would he need to apologize to you, Josie?"

Chapter Twelve

Josie's worst nightmare had come true. Now Tobias would know her dark secret and her great shame. Would she have to leave again and never see her family? Give up on seeing Dinah grow up? Or, worse, would Drew's parents take Dinah and never let her return to them?

"Josie?"

She looked up and into Tobias's eyes. He deserved the truth. She would hurt him again, but at least he could move on knowing he had done nothing wrong.

Tobias pulled up a chair and took her hands into his. "You have to tell me everything."

"I do not want to, but, yes, now I have no choice."

"What did he do?" Tobias asked, the tone of his voice edged with anger.

Josie took in a shuddering breath. "It was at that big party at his house a few weeks before Christmas. He always flirted with me and said vile things about you and me and how we were so square and not cool."

Tobias's hands squeezed hers. "I told him not to tease you in that way. What else did he do?"

When she tried to look away, Tobias touched a finger to her chin so she had to look into his eyes. "Tell me."

She took in another gulp of air, her lungs burning with the need to scream, her heartbeat throbbing through her pulse. "He gave me a glass of punch then told me you were looking for me." She stopped, the memories as bright as the red geraniums blooming in a huge pot by the pool. "He pointed to the back of the house, so I went to find you. He followed me."

Tobias let go of her hands and stood, his elbows bent, his hands on his hips. "What did he do, Josie?"

"The drink had something in it. I only took one or two sips, but it made me dizzy and I felt sick. He pushed me into a room and… I couldn't get away, Tobias. I couldn't get away."

Tobias stared at her as if he hadn't heard correctly. But realization covered him in a rush of bright anger that darkened his cheeks and changed his expression into a hard-edged, grisly acceptance. He backed away and went to the glass door leading out onto the terrace.

Leaning his forehead against the glass, he shuddered. "No," he said, his voice rising. "No."

Josie held her hands to her face, her head falling as she tried to hide her shame and the horror of what had happened. The vivid memories she'd tried so hard to bury came back in full-forced clarity. "I'm sorry. I did not want you to know. I couldn't tell you."

"So you left me?" he said, his voice rising as he turned to face her. "You left me and let me believe the worst—that you didn't love me, that I had failed you?"

"I had no choice," she said, her body numb with pain and grief. "I had no choice. I didn't think you'd love *me* anymore if you knew."

He stood pressed against the door in the same way she'd stood when she'd gone to see him in her old home. "You didn't trust me enough to tell me? You know I would have done anything to protect you, to make this up to you."

"I was afraid of that, afraid you might confront him and he'd lie to you. I barely remember it happening because he drugged me and he was drunk, Tobias. So drunk that he didn't even remember my name or that we'd been in that room."

Tobias paced in front of her. "You found me that night, told me you weren't feeling well. Why didn't you tell me what had happened?"

"I was in shock and terrified," she said,

each word dropping like a pebble against glass. "Afraid of his power and money, his friends who made fun of me, of how you'd react and what you might do to him."

"So you decided you'd just run away. We could have worked this out and we could have still gotten married. I... I would have listened and understood."

"Think long and hard on that," she said, standing to face him as she found her courage. "Would you have been able to get past it and still marry me?"

Tobias stopped and stared at her, his eyes misty and red rimmed, his expression grim and defeated. "I would have done anything, anything, Josie, to keep you with me."

She nodded and then she put a hand to her stomach. "Even accept another man's child as your own?"

Tobias felt a rushing roar inside his head. He'd been angry in his life, but nothing like this. This was a rage that made him want to break every window in this room, made him want to find Drew Benington and tear him apart.

But that was not the Amish way.

How did he deal with this now? How did he keep moving, working, living, trying to have the life he'd been denied? How, when a man he considered his friend had betrayed him and Josie in such a callous, horrible way? Why had Tobias forced her to go to that party, knowing she felt uncomfortable among those rich *Englisch* teenagers?

This was on him. All those years he'd wondered, and it was his fault, after all, that she'd left.

"You wanted the truth," she said on a raw whisper, taking his silence as a condemnation. "Now you have it. Dinah is my child and that is why I had to leave. I would not shame you into marrying me out of a sense of duty. I had to leave, and when I came back to this area, things got bad, and out of desperation, I left my baby on Raesha and Naomi's porch."

Tobias couldn't speak. The thought of

her out there alone in the cold of winter, pregnant and afraid, made him want to rush to her and hold her tight. But the thought of her not trusting him to help her or still love her held him away.

Why had God brought him here to find her only to have this happen? The Beningtons showing up so she was forced to admit what she'd kept from him? Was that *Gott*'s plan?

Maybe it had to be this way so they both were forced to see the real truth.

"I do not understand why you went to such extremes."

"I left my child with two women I'd trusted before, and then I became ill with grief and longing and loneliness. I caught pneumonia and almost died, but *Gott* had other plans for me. My brother came back here to sell our place, and he went to the neighbors' to let them know he'd be over there renovating the house and barn."

Tobias wiped at his eyes and nodded. "What else happened?"

Josie wrapped her arms around her

stomach in a protective stance. "Josiah noticed the pink hat Dinah was wearing and knew immediately it had to be mine." She paused and swallowed away the grief. "I carried that little bonnet with me everywhere. It was the only thing I had left from my *mamm*. But I wanted Dinah to have it, to keep her warm."

Tobias closed his eyes and then blinked. "How did Josiah find you?"

"He'd been searching for me—hired Nathan Craig to find me once he lost touch with me after I left Kentucky. But I was still out there trying to hide, sick and hoping I'd die."

Tobias closed his eyes again, thanked God she had not died. "I'm glad he found you."

"It took a while," she said, nodding. "But, yes, Nathan located me in a nearby hospital and Josiah brought me to the Bawell place. But I was so dead inside, I wouldn't tell anyone the truth." She took a long breath. "I was mean to everyone and caused a lot of trouble, but Naomi and

Judy Campton helped me find my way again."

Judy Campton. So she had to have known all of this, but she couldn't blurt it out to him. And here he stood in what used to be her home. Ironic that he was back here with Josie.

"You told Josiah that Dinah was your child?"

"Yes, but they had already found proof," she said. "DNA from Josiah and Dinah showed he was related to Dinah. That's why he was able to keep her with him even before he found me. But I didn't want anything to do with her after I came back. She reminded me too much of... Drew."

Tobias sank down on a padded floral stool, exhaustion and shock overcoming him. "So here we are. You have a child and you left me because of what Drew did. I'd say he owes you a lot more than an apology."

Josie lowered her head. "I am shocked that he asked his parents to do this. He can't come but sending them is harsh. He's even more of a coward than I thought and I hope he never gets out of prison."

Tobias only now remembered people were waiting in the other room. "They were about to tell me everything."

"I had to find you," she said. "You needed to hear this from me."

Anger stiffened his spine. "You were forced or I would have never known."

"I'm sorry. I wanted to tell you," she said, her tone quiet and defeated. "I was about to the other day at the festival, but then Nathan showed up. Either way, I've hurt you. I will always regret that."

Tobias let things settle in his head. Then he looked back at Josie and motioned toward the front of the big house. "Do they know about the child?"

Josie put a hand to her mouth, her eyes burning with a solid fear. "I don't know, but...they might have figured it out since I went to them before I ran away. They didn't believe me then, but what if they came to find out? That's the other reason I had to tell you. They might try to take

Dinah away from us. I will not let that happen."

Tobias stood. "You need to know something, Josie. They told me Drew is dying of liver cancer. That is the reason he sent them to find both of us."

Josie gasped and seemed to shrink away. "He wants atonement before he dies."

"*Ja*, so it seems. I am glad he didn't show up here. I am not sure how I would have handled that."

Tobias reached out his hand. "I need to get back in there. Will you *kumm*?"

"I… I don't think that is such a *gut* idea."

Before he could convince her, Jewel came out into the sunroom, her gaze apologetic. "Josie, your brother came to check on you. Now Alisha is asking that you all come into the conference room."

"Josie?" Tobias reached out to her again. "I'm with you now. We have to stand together."

Josie didn't look so sure. "You are not angry at me?"

"I am angry," he admitted, "at you, at

Drew for what he did, at myself for being so naive and for the time we've wasted when we could have worked this out somehow."

Josie's expression showed her torment, her cheeks flushed, her eyes downcast. "I am so sorry, Tobias. So sorry."

"We will talk about sorry later," he said. "Right now we need to go into that room and face Drew's parents. Together."

She took his hand in a tentative silence and Tobias breathed a sigh of relief, only to be followed by a deep sense of dread. His world had shifted, his faith had been sorely tested, and the enraged anger he felt clutched him so tightly he thought he might suffocate.

But now he knew what she'd tried so hard to hide, and somehow he had to accept what had happened and reconcile that with what might have been.

Or what could come now that the healing would begin.

I need strength. I need to talk to someone. I need Gott's *help.*

The woman he had loved from the moment he'd met her had not trusted that love enough to share the worst time of her life with him. Now he had to accept that a man he'd befriended in his running-around time had ruined Josie and ruined their plans for a future together. She had a child by another man and she'd given that child to her brother. He knew she'd made that sacrifice for the sake of the child. Josie had put Dinah on the Bawell porch for a reason. Josiah had told Tobias that the Bawells had helped her as a child, when she was living in fear. She must have felt they would give Dinah a good, safe life. But he had to grasp the question burning inside his head. Did she love Dinah or was she just tolerating the *kinder*?

Because he now knew who little Dinah had reminded him of the one time he'd seen her.

Drew. Dinah reminded him of Drew.

How would either of them get past that?

Chapter Thirteen

Josie did not want to go into that room, but Tobias held her hand, obviously not caring about rules or decorum at this point.

Josiah came out of the office near the conference room. "Josie, I was growing concerned."

Jewel stood between them. "I explained what's going on to Josiah. Let Josiah go in with you, Josie. He is your brother, after all, and he knows what needs to be said."

Josiah gave Josie a questioning glance.

"Tobias knows the truth now, *bruder*," she said, her throat raw and her head pounding. "All of it."

Josiah glanced from her to Tobias. "I will go in if you both agree. But Dinah is my child now."

Tobias indicated a nod. "I think that would be in Josie's best interest. After all, you are Dinah's legal father, *ja*?"

"I am," Josiah said, appreciation and regret in his eyes.

Josie could see Tobias had become a man overnight and now he'd grown even stronger. Then again, the news he'd just learned could do that to a person.

He'd held her hand, but could he truly forgive her? She'd seen the hurt in his eyes when he'd finally realized the truth. That also meant he realized she'd kept this a secret for well over three years. Years of lost time between them. Too long for secrets between them. What if they couldn't repair the damage she'd done?

No more secrets, she decided. Here and now, she would face the truth and try to be strong, as Naomi had taught her.

Giving Tobias a glimpse that she hoped

showed that courage, she indicated she was ready.

He opened the door and guided her into the room. Josiah followed behind.

Josie stood just inside the door, her gaze moving over Nathan's sympathetic face and Alisha's concerned frown. They had worked so hard to make sure Dinah was safe and protected.

Then she glanced over at Drew's parents. His mother's eyes were as red and swollen as Josie's had to be. His dad looked haggard and beaten by the world.

Her heart went out to them. They had no way of knowing what Drew had done to her, and they'd refused to believe her the one time she'd tried to talk to them. But someone had stepped forward to make him pay. Now he had a horrible disease that couldn't be hushed or hidden away. A disease that no amount of power could overcome.

She should feel some type of vindication. Instead, Josie felt sad and full of pain and regret. She'd have to forgive him—not so much for his sake, but because that was the Amish way and she needed the peace of mind that forgiveness brought.

"Josie," Alisha said, rising to take her arm. "I'm glad you came." Then she looked at Tobias. "Are you both okay?"

Tobias nodded, but didn't look okay. "*Ja*. Josie told me everything."

"And what is everything?" Drew's father asked as he stood.

Nathan motioned him back in his seat. "I think Josie is ready to talk to you two. Is that why you came, Josie?"

Josie shook her head. "*Neh*, I came to find Tobias." Then she faced the Beningtons. "Tobias told me about Drew. I am sorry. I understand he had a message for me."

Drew's mother wiped at her eyes while Alisha guided Josie and Tobias to their chairs. Josiah found a seat off to the side.

"Drew did some horrible things and now he's in prison," his mother said, her gaze on Josie. "He's trying to make amends before…before he dies. We hope to bring him home soon, if the parole board will agree to an early release."

Josie wondered if Drew was truly sorry or if he only wanted to get out of prison and die at home. She brushed that doubt aside and took the high road. "I hope you can do that."

Tobias still looked shell-shocked. "Josie told me what Drew did to her and why she was forced to leave Orchard Mountain. I had no idea. She did not want me to know, but she felt she had to tell me the truth."

Mr. Benington let out an angry huff of breath, his expression hardening. His wife grasped his hand. "Theodore, we came here for a purpose. Don't chide her now. Drew made it clear he wanted Josephine to know that he is sorry. So very sorry."

Tobias stared them down. "Chide her? She did nothing wrong. It seems to me Drew is the culprit here, and apologizing won't change that."

"He made mistakes," Drew's mother said. "He *is* serving his time. We are so sorry, Josephine. You came to us and tried to make us see, but we didn't want to believe the worst of our only child."

Josie couldn't speak. They did remember her coming to see them. Did they remember what she had told them?

"Look," Nathan said. "Now that we're all here, and we have Alisha's law expertise to guide us, let's put it all on the table." He narrowed his gaze on the couple. "You've delivered the messages from Drew. Josie and Tobias at least know now that he regrets what he did. His actions hurt both of them. What more do you need to say?"

Drew's father cleared his throat and stared at Josie. Then he said the words she'd dreaded since Nathan had come to the festival booth. "Did you have Drew's child, Josie? If you did, we'd like to see our grandchild."

Tobias watched Josie's face for a reaction. Her gaze landed first on him and then her brother. "I... I don't know how to answer that question."

"A simple yes or no will suffice," Mr. Benington replied, his tone quiet but firm. "You blurted that out to us and then you ran out the door."

Josiah moved forward and put a hand on Josie's shoulder. Josie took in a calming breath. She looked pale and distraught. Tobias wanted to help her, to protect her, but he had to let her tell this story.

Josie lifted her shoulders and looked over at Drew's parents. "I did have Drew's child. A little girl."

Pamela Benington began to sob. "Oh, my. Oh, I can't believe this. Josie, I'm so sorry, but…we have a granddaughter."

"No, *I* had a child," Josie replied. "A child I had to give up."

"What?" Theodore Benington glared across at Josie. "You gave her up for adoption?"

"I had no choice," Josie said, her voice growing stronger with each word. "But I put her in the best home I could find."

"Where is she?" Pamela said, still crying. "We have to see her."

Josiah held up his hand, palm up. "Dinah is with my wife and me. We adopted her. Raesha and I fell in love a few months after Dinah and Josie came to us. I saw Dinah first and recognized the pink baby bonnet she was wearing. It had Josie's initials stitched inside. I questioned Raesha and Naomi, and they admitted the child had been left on their porch."

He explained who the Bawell women were and how they'd watched after Dinah until he could prove he was her *onkel*.

"They became instant nannies to little Dinah, and Raesha and I fell in love. After we married, we officially adopted her."

Theodore hit his hand on the table and then pointed at Josie. "You left our granddaughter on someone's porch?"

"Not just anyone's porch," Josiah continued while Tobias fisted his hands to keep from lashing out at Drew's irrational father. "The Bawell porch. Two good women who had plenty of love to give a child."

When Theodore tried to speak, Tobias responded. "Let him explain."

Josiah took a breath and continued. "When I found out through a DNA test the child Raesha and Naomi were taking care of was related to me, I searched for Josie. My sister was very ill in a nearby hospital. Nathan helped me locate her and bring her home." He stopped and looked at Josie. "Josie came to live with us, but she gave up her rights as a mother. Dinah is our daughter now—mine and Raesha's."

Alisha leaned forward, her shoulder-length hair falling around her face. "I went exactly by the book in helping them to adopt Dinah." Then she crossed her hands on the table. "But the Amish have their own way of taking in children. They don't ask questions, and they make sure the child is safe and well cared for."

"Our son didn't agree to that kind of dubious law," Theodore said.

"He never signed the birth certificate," Josie replied. "Your son didn't even remember what happened."

"He wasn't given the chance to sign," Drew's father retorted.

"But he has a child," Pamela said. "We're related to her, too. We should have been informed."

Alisha jotted notes. "After Josiah and Raesha were married, I contacted your son at his college, Mr. Benington. They wanted to formally adopt Dinah, and Josie had agreed. But Drew refused to believe the truth, so he said he didn't care and wanted no part of this. He wouldn't sign a VAP—Voluntary Acknowledgment of Paternity. I think by then two other girls had come forward, but he was still in denial and refused to sign any paperwork that could implicate him in a crime." She stopped for a pause, then added, "Later, of course, he went on trial for those two attacks."

"He never told us about this situation and it didn't come out at the trial," Drew's father said. "But he could still claim rights."

Alisha nodded. "Yes, *he* could, but we'd

have to go through a lot of paperwork and legalese. As you told us, we're running out of time."

Josiah cleared his throat. "My wife and I love Dinah. She is happy and healthy. Josie helps out with her and our son, Daniel. We'd hate to lose our daughter."

"Our granddaughter," Pamela reminded them. "I'd like to see her."

Her husband took her hand. "Honey, we'll talk to our own legal team and see what can be done, but Drew won't be able to raise her and he might not even get to see her before he dies."

"We could raise her," Pamela said. "We can give her anything she needs or wants."

"She has everything she needs," Josie said. "You can't do that to my family."

Tobias took her hand. "You've said what you came to say. Josie is tired and I have a job to get back to." He looked toward Nathan. "Are we finished?"

Nathan gave the Beningtons a long stare. "For now, I think."

"I'd like to see my granddaughter," Pamela insisted. "I promise I won't say or do anything to frighten her. I just need to see her. Just this once until…until we can decide how to handle this."

Josiah almost spoke, but Alisha shot both him and Tobias a warning glance.

"We'll be in touch," she said to the Beningtons. "Thank you both for coming. Meantime, I'll go back over the law and check all the steps we took again. For now, Dinah is legally adopted by the Fishers. It will be up to them if you can see Dinah before you go."

After they all moved outside, Josiah motioned to Josie. "We should go and tell Raesha what's happened."

Josie nodded, too shocked and confused to argue with her brother.

Tobias stopped him. "I need to talk to Josie. If you don't mind, I'll borrow Abram's buggy and drive her home."

Josiah's frown indicated he didn't like that. "Josie?"

Josie looked from her brother to Tobias. "It's all right, Josiah. I'll be all right."

Reluctantly Josiah headed to the buggy. Her brother probably wished he'd never found her at all. They could be raising Dinah without all of this drama she'd brought with her.

Tobias touched her shoulder. "*Kumm* with me. I'll explain to Abram. It's a slow day anyway, so he'll understand."

"What will you tell him?" she asked, hoping word wouldn't spread about the Beningtons being here.

"That I need a couple of hours with my best girl," he said. Then he stalked away, the joy that endearment used to hold no longer in his voice.

Chapter Fourteen

"Take as long as you want," Abram had
told Tobias earlier. "Tobias, are you all
right? I am here to help with whatever
you need."

"Just your horse and buggy. After Josie
and I talk, I'll need to take her home."

Abram nodded. "Later, if you want to
unload what's really going on, I am a *gut*
listener and I do not repeat what is said to
me in confidence."

"I do owe you an explanation and I will
give one, later."

Now Tobias sat in the park with Josie,
hidden from the street by a big hedge and

a mushrooming oak tree. The sky, so blue and perfect, didn't know of the turmoil in his heart. *Gott* had to know, but right now, the world seemed surreal and like a dream. Josie—his Josie—had a child. She was a mother, though she did not actually mother this child. So she was more of an aunt to Dinah?

"This is confusing," he finally said. "A lot to take in."

Josie sat with her hands clutched in her lap. "I have caused a lot of people so much heartache," she said. "I acted out because I was angry that Josiah had left me in that house. But I had no idea what that had cost him. He went to Ohio, seeking help from my *mamm*'s family. At first, they believed he had just run away and wanted to be free. But Josiah stayed Amish. Barely had a *rumspringa*. But they treated him, and later me, very badly. After the barn fire, he came back and took me with him, and for a while life was better. But they blamed us for not telling them about how cruel our *daed* had become."

Tobias tried to imagine what she'd been through. "So your *daed* was mean?"

"Ja," she said. Then she sat silent for a moment. "He would pick fights about anything. Our *mamm* shielded us from his wrath, but...he took it out on her. So many times." She looked up and to the east, where her old home was located. "I used to show up at the Bawells', making excuses. We needed sugar or flour or I fell and scratched my knee and I didn't want to wake my mom."

Tobias couldn't imagine a little girl living like that. "You were brave, Josie. You've always been brave."

She turned and stared over at him, her eyes brimming with pain and dark memories. "I am not so brave, Tobias. It is my fault that my parents died."

Tobias didn't think this day could get any worse. "What do you mean?"

She kept her gaze on him. "They were fighting out in the barn. My *mamm* went out there to tell him supper was ready. He wanted supper on the table at a certain time. I don't know what happened, but he became angry and started shouting at her." Josie took a long breath and clutched her hands tighter together. "I grabbed a lamp since it was getting dark and ran out to the barn, but when I saw him grabbing her, I tripped and dropped the lamp. The hay caught on fire and then my mother screamed for me to run. I stood and called for her. 'Mamm, Mamm!'"

Tobias took her hand. "Josie, you don't need to tell me."

"No, I do. I have to. No more secrets, Tobias. No more."

He held her hand, his eyes following the panic rising up in her like a dark cloud. "Josie—tell me, then."

"I called for her and she tried to run to me, but he held her there. He held her with fire all around them. I ran for help, but when I got back it was too late. Too late to save either of them."

Tobias pulled her close. "You never told me. I am so sorry."

"It is hard to see it all again. But in

my mind, late at night, I see it and then I dream that horrible dream of hearing my own screams, of watching that fire surround my mother." She sobbed against his shirt. "I ran to the Bawell house, and Mr. Bawell and his son went over to help. But it was too late. I stayed there until Josiah could come and get me."

Tobias held her, his heart beating along with hers. "You have suffered enough, Josie. Enough."

She pulled away and wiped her eyes. "Now you know my secrets. Josiah didn't even know about me dropping the lamp. I came home after Josiah found me in the hospital, but I couldn't take being back in Campton Creek and seeing Dinah being raised by someone else. I tried to take Dinah and run again, but I wound up hiding upstairs at the old place. Josiah found me and that's when I told him the truth. I blamed myself for the deaths of my parents."

"But he did not send you away. He understands it was not your fault."

"He got me help," she said. "Judy Campton helped me understand that I cannot carry that blame for the rest of my life. But after Drew, my blame and the shame of what he'd done to me almost did me in forever."

She touched a hand to Tobias's jaw. "I stare at that house every evening when I'm sitting on the side porch. Stare and remember things I've tried to forget. And one night a few weeks ago, I thought I saw you standing there on the porch and now I know it was you."

Tobias could see how that had caused her to have a setback of massive proportions. "That is part of why you don't want me living next door. That and… Dinah. You knew I'd see Drew in her features."

"I did not want you living there because I did not want you to know all of the awful things I've done."

"Things that were done to you, Josie. People who were cruel to you. How can I blame you for that?"

She dropped her hand. "But you do

blame me for not being honest with you, don't you?"

Tobias couldn't deny that. "It's not blame. It's regret.Regret that you could not trust me enough to tell me what had happened. We could have worked through this together, for our purpose, for *Gott*'s purpose."

A blush moved over her face. "Could have? But not now. Now it's over for us, isn't it, Tobias?"

Tobias couldn't answer that question. "I have much to think about, Josie," he admitted. "I came here with *one* purpose, to find you and hear what had happened."

Her eyelashes fluttered as she blinked away tears. "And now that you've accomplished that?"

Tobias stood and paced underneath the sheltering oak. "Now I want to buy that house and…be near you. That is what I want right now."

Josie stood and gazed into his eyes. "I won't stop you buying the house if that is truly what you want. Why you'd want to stay after all of this, I cannot understand."

"I'm staying because I have no one waiting for me back in Kentucky, and I have nowhere else to go."

"I hope you won't regret that."

The disappointment and despair in her eyes ripped through his heart. "I regret that I wasn't able to protect you. I will be here, waiting, whenever you feel that you can trust me and love me again."

"What if that never happens, Tobias? I am damaged, scared, afraid to leave the house most days. I don't know how I could be a wife to any man."

"Then I will still be near you. And that has to count for something, ain't so?"

Josie bobbed her head and didn't speak.

"I will take you home now," he said. "You must be tired."

"I am," she said. "And I want to talk to Josiah and Raesha. They cannot lose Dinah. None of us want to lose Dinah."

Tobias could see that Josie loved the little girl.

But that would always be between them. The reminder of the boy he'd considered a friend doing such a vile thing to the woman Tobias loved.

They might not ever get past that, but with *Gott*'s grace, Tobias planned to try.

Exhaustion tugged at Josie as she went to open the back door to the main house. Knowing her family would be waiting for her, she almost turned to go back to the *grossmammi haus*. The old Josie would have done that, but today she'd become a new person. A person who'd been through the worst and was still standing. Tobias knew all of her secrets, and he'd seen all of her flaws. Maybe he'd decide he needed to move on.

She'd stood up to Drew's parents, the people who'd scorned her and accused her of only wanting their son's prestige and money. Now they'd been forced to see him for what he was, the same way she'd seen him from the first time she'd met him.

She'd never dreamed his ways would

ruin her life with such terrible destruction. But now she had family to protect her. Maybe she'd be able to forgive him and let her faith carry her through. Stopping, her hand on the doorknob, she couldn't help looking over toward the old place. When she saw a horse and buggy in the winding drive, she knew Tobias was there. He walked up onto the porch.

And waved at her.

So close she could run over there and hold him in her arms.

So far away she couldn't touch that place inside his heart that she had pierced and shattered with her fears and deceit.

"I will find a way to win you back," she whispered, thinking she'd been foolish to fight this. "No matter what."

Then she went inside to face her family.

They were waiting, a plate of uneaten sandwiches on the table, a pitcher of fresh lemonade on the sideboard.

"I'm not hungry," Josie said.

"Neither are we," Naomi replied. "Your

brother told us what happened in town. How are you dealing with this, Josie?"

Josie poured some lemonade into a glass, her hands trembling. "I've had to relive all of the worst times of my life, so I'm not great."

She sank down on the high-backed chair next to Josiah. He hadn't spoken a word to her. "I am so sorry that I brought this on all of you."

Naomi held up a finger. "You did not bring anything on anyone. You were betrayed and wronged, your life ruined. Maybe you didn't make wise choices, but *Gott* always knows the outcome. He brought you home, Josie. Home, where you need to be."

Josiah nodded, his dark eyes full of pain. "He also brought Dinah to us and, now, Tobias. This is something we should consider."

Josie glanced at their faces. "You have been discussing this, *ja*?"

Raesha glanced at her husband. "We

have enough to worry about right now. These people could take Dinah away."

Naomi shot Josie a warning glance. "We will not fret about that. She belongs here with us and we will pray on that."

"Isn't that what you've been discussing?" Josie asked, confused and weary. "I don't want Dinah to go away. You all must know that."

"We do," Raesha replied. "We all love her."

Josiah stood up. "I talked to Tobias briefly after he dropped you off earlier. He still wants to buy the house, Josie. How do you feel about that?"

"We talked about it," she said, "and I told him I would not stop him. But he has accepted that he and I can never be more than friends."

"Accepted?" Naomi looked skeptical.

Josie set down the half-finished glass of lemonade, the syrupy, honeyed sweetness of the drink making her feel ill. "I think I've lost Tobias. I knew this would happen and now it has. I should be glad that he finally sees me for what I am. He might still want the house, *bruder.* But he does not want me anymore."

He wanted this house and he wanted Josie here with him. Hopeful after he'd talked to Josiah in the driveway of the Bawell property, half an hour later Tobias found himself at the Fisher house and wondered if he truly still wanted the same things he'd come here to find.

A home to call his own? Yes, he still wanted that.

A family of his own? No doubt about that.

Josie?

He'd stopped there on the porch when he caught a movement on the breezeway across from the footbridge.

Josie, headed to the main house. How did his heart always sense her presence before his head caught up?

She stopped and stood so still she could have been a dream only.

But she was real and she had been

through the kind of trauma that most did not return from.

Gott's will, he reminded himself.

In an instant, she had gone inside. Tobias stood there in the sweet wind and wished he could go back in time and change all the things that had brought him here.

But he couldn't erase becoming Drew's friend or falling in love with Josephine Fisher. And he couldn't erase the awful consequences of talking her into going to that fancy Christmas party when she had not wanted to do so.

He had caused this turn of events, maybe because he had turned away from his faith in the blink of an eye and, just like that, bad things had begun to happen.

Gott's will or his own selfish pride?

Tobias watched the Bawell house, the afternoon sun radiating through the trees like a beacon, the hot wind moving over his skin while he remembered that chilly winter when he'd lost the woman he loved.

When he saw Josie running out of the

main house, her head down, his first instinct was to go to her and comfort her.

But he held back, remembering the revelations this day had brought. Did she blame him for everything that had transpired since the last time he'd seen her? Was that why she'd told him to leave when she'd found him here in the house?

Tobias watched as she went straight into the *grossmammi haus*, and then he reluctantly got back into Abram's buggy and headed toward town. By the time he got back, the day would be almost done. And he might be out of a job.

Defeated, Tobias had a feeling he'd be moving on soon enough anyway. He couldn't make Josie love him if she could never forgive him for taking her to that party. If her family lost little Dinah, none of them would ever get over it.

Chapter Fifteen

❧

"So now you know the whole story."

Tobias waited for Beth's and Abram's reactions as they both sat quietly in their favorite chairs, Beth knitting and Abram tugging at his beard.

Tobias sat across from them, wondering how he'd managed to mess things up so badly. He should have stayed in Kentucky, unknowing and lonely. That which he'd believed to be hurt could not compare to the jagged, sharp pain of despair he now held in his heart. The blame of his part in Josie's tragedy held him like a prison, causing him to stare at a piece of wood for ten minutes and then not be able to create anything out of it.

What right did he have to create anything meaningful in this world? He'd failed the woman he planned to have a life with. He should have protected her and kept her safe.

Beth put down her knitting and glanced at her husband. "Are you going to speak or should I?"

Abram's eyebrows formed a V over his nose. "What would you have me say?"

Tobias braced himself. Was he about to be kicked out of their home and be out of a job again?

Beth made a clucking noise. "Tobias, we had heard things about the babe that was found on the Bawell porch and how Josie came to be here. But the *blabbermauls* soon quieted down once Josie confessed all and asked for forgiveness. Forgiveness that she didn't actually need since this happened against her will. But she wanted a fresh start, and so she confessed to taking a wayward path. We refused to spread any rumors since she has returned to the fold and she seems to be putting her life back together." Beth worked her knitting needles. "Dinah is a beautiful little girl."

Tobias saw the sincerity in Beth's gray eyes. *"Denke,"* he said. "Josie has been shamed enough. She has been hiding away at the Bawell place, and then I showed up and scared her back into hiding even more." Shrugging, he dropped his head. "She'd finally begun to attend gatherings more, but this latest might set her back. I feel like I'm to blame for that."

He wanted to add he was to blame for all of Josie's troubles.

"You came for all the right reasons," Abram pointed out. "Everything has brought you to this moment. So don't go blaming yourself for anything."

Tobias shook his head, wondering if Abram could see his guilt. *"Ja,* but look at me. I'm a for-sure mess and I messed up things for Josie when I made her mingle in the *Englisch* world."

"Josie has a mind of her own," Beth said. "She didn't have to go to that party."

"She is strong now, but back then she was searching for something, and she was innocent and naive. I tried to change her and I made a big mistake. We would be married today if I had not tried so hard to blend in with the *Englisch*."

Abram removed his reading glasses. "I believe you have both learned a hard lesson, but you are also both more mature now."

Tobias tried not to let his frustrations show, but he must have made a horrible frown. Beth sent her husband a worried glance. "State your point, Abram."

Abram took his time while seconds ticked by. "Josie is here and single. You are here and single. I'd say *Gott* worked to bring you both together again, because now you're both done with running-around time, and you are mature and wise beyond your years."

"Wise but not together, Abram. I doubt we will ever be together again."

Abram shook his head. "You are together—you are both together here. If you buy the Fisher place, you'll be almost as together as two people can be."

"But not really together," Beth cautioned, "although I do see your point, husband."

Tobias stood and shook his head. "I'm confused."

Beth gave him a sympathetic glance. "Life is confusing at times, but you have everything you want right here. Do not waste any more time filled with regrets and doubts, Tobias. Fight the good fight. Make Josie love you again, despite the guilt you both carry. Why come all this way just to give up now?"

"*Ja*, that is what I was trying to say," Abram agreed, proud of himself. "You two belong together."

Tobias went to his room and thought about how Beth and Abram had taken him in and fed him. They'd also nurtured that empty spot in his soul. He could never repay them, but he thanked *Gott* he'd found them.

Keeping thanking Gott.

The voice in his head told him he might be moving in the right direction even if everything felt wrong. How could he be sure? He wondered if the Beningtons would make trouble for them. Tobias didn't see any way out of that.

Chalking up Beth's and Abram's determined suggestions as just wishful thinking, he decided he'd bide his time and see what happened next. Josie would have to make the next move, but with all of this going on, he was afraid she'd shut down again. She had shut him out completely and now he understood why.

Her memories of their time together were tangled up with the pain of how her life had turned out. How could they ever find their way back to each other?

Two days had passed and no one had heard a word from the Beningtons. Josie wanted to take a breath of relief, but she feared this was the quiet before the storm.

She wondered about Tobias. She had not talked to him since that awful morning in the sunroom. Should she reach out to him?

No. He knew the truth now. She'd seen the doubt and disappointment on his face. He wouldn't be able to get past this and forgive her since she'd left him without an explanation.

And refused to tell him the truth until she'd been forced.

Josie stood on the breezeway and studied the dark clouds on the horizon, but she had to go to the main house and help Raesha with food and cleaning.

Raesha had already planned a quilt frolic this afternoon, and Josie felt she should be there since they'd already invited everyone. No one here felt like quilting, but Naomi had told them they could not cancel it since they'd planned it weeks ago.

"It will take our minds off the things we cannot change nor predict," Naomi had announced, making it hard for Raesha and Josie to sit idle. "We must continue on and set people straight if they bring it up."

Someone would manage to ask pointed questions. Josie only had one question. She wondered if Drew's parents were still in Campton Creek. They'd been insistent about seeing Dinah.

But when she'd voiced her worries last night at dinner, her brother had frowned and left the house.

Naomi told her Josiah acted as most men did in times of trouble. He took refuge out in the fields and in the barn. But Josie had to wonder if her brother was tired of the drama and scandal she'd brought into his life.

Josiah used to tell Josie that because of her he'd found the woman meant to be his wife. Why had something so wonderful *gut* had to happen because of something so horribly wrong?

She couldn't get anyone to talk to her about this, so they all went about their lives as usual.

The frolic was still on, and while they worried they also worked. That was how things were done around here. And on days when they had quilting frolics, Raesha left the hat shop early and her assistants took over.

Josie enjoyed the timeless art of stitching patterns and colors into something tangible and useful. She could see life in their handmade quilts, all patterns and squares and bright colors, coming together to form something beautiful.

Gott's work in every stitch. That was what Naomi always said. And although Mammi's eyes couldn't see to stitch, she sat with them when they did and regaled them with her wisdom and wit. She always encouraged when someone messed up a stitch.

"It doesn't have to be perfect," she'd say. "We are not perfect. Only *Gott* is."

Perfection. Josie had always dreamed of the perfect family, the perfect home with perfect children.

Naomi was right. There was no such thing.

Life didn't need to be all wonderful to be life, she decided. She'd been forgiven by her community and by *Gott*. What more did she need?

She wanted Tobias to forgive her for not turning to him.

Josie needed the distraction of stitching and laughing, that was what she needed. She had not been sleeping well, and each time she finally fell asleep, she had dreams of someone ripping Dinah out of her arms.

That nightmare could come true at any time now if the Beningtons found a way around the law.

Tobias held the chisel against the wood, determined to make another leg so the stool he had in mind would be balanced and precise. The tall, heavy stool wouldn't stand on just three legs, after all. He'd measured and shaped, using an air compressor to run the band saw. After making the cut, he'd started gouging the line into the wood so he could form a tenon to meet the mortise. The tenon and mortise would hold the corner of the stool's seat to all four legs. He'd take an awl to mark and make the spot where he'd add the special glue Abram used to secure the tenon joints.

This particular stool—called an Amish folding step stool—would serve well in any kitchen. He could almost picture an Amish woman sitting on the high stool, peeling potatoes or snapping beans and then turning to use it as a stepladder by pulling out the small retractable steps hinged underneath the seat. This one was made from solid oak that would be sanded and varnished to a dark burnished goldenbrown sheen.

Josie came to mind, as she did most of the day and night. Why couldn't he let her go?

Maybe because he'd traveled hundreds of miles to find her, and now that he had he was too stubborn to give up? Most men would have by now, and especially after all the things he'd heard during the last few days.

Two days since his world had crumbled with each new revelation. Two days ago, he'd only wanted to love Josie and know why she'd left him.

Now he knew the truth and it stuck in his throat like a brittle bone. What she'd been through no woman should have to endure. Tobias didn't know how to get around everything that now stood between them. So he kept whittling and shaving, using the wood to keep his thoughts centered and precise.

"Do not gouge that leg to the bone, Tobias," Abram cautioned as he hurried by carrying a two-by-four cut from pine. "Else that stool will look kind of funny and tilt to the left a bit too much."

Tobias stopped and stared at the wood he had braced on the saw table. "You stopped me just in time."

"You were not focusing on the carving," Abram replied, his tone soft. "But once you get it together, that will be a mighty fine step stool that anyone should be proud to have in their kitchen."

Why did he get the feeling Abram wasn't just encouraging him about his talent? The man wanted what was best for Tobias and he would forever be grateful for that.

But he'd need a lot of tools to figure out the next step in his life. He loved Josie. That would never change. But could they work things out between them? A marriage shouldn't start this way—with sad, tragic memories hovering between the bride and groom.

How could he fix this?

In a million little ways.

That was what Jewel, Judy and Bettye had suggested. He didn't have much time left to win over Josie. The house was waiting, but would she ever want to live there again? Would it be fair to her to make her live in a house that had brought her only fear and pain and nightmare memories?

He had to put this out of his mind for now.

Tobias worked on the stool the rest of the afternoon. The work did help his mind to settle. Maybe he'd carve some more trinkets. Those had sold well at the festival and now Abram had made a shelf in the showroom for what he called Tobias's toys.

"I could use more carved horses and maybe a couple buggies," he'd told Tobias this morning. "The flowers and wooden dolls go over well with the women, of course." Then he'd chuckled. "Your whittling fingers are going to be tired, for sure."

Tired would be good to Tobias. Maybe he'd sleep so deeply he wouldn't dream of things he could not have.

He and Abram were closing up for the day, the other workers waving as they left for home, some on foot and some picked up by cars or buggies. Tobias always stayed back to help since he rode home with Abram every day anyway.

When they heard the front doorbell jingle, Tobias turned from tallying receipts to find Jewel hurrying toward him, her eyes bright.

"Oh, good, you're still here," she said, eyeing Tobias.

"Jewel, what's wrong?"

"The Beningtons, that's what's wrong," Jewel said under her breath.

"It's all right," Tobias said. "Abram knows all about what is going on."

Abram nodded. "*Ja*, I do, but I'll give you two some privacy."

He shuffled toward the workroom.

Jewel stared over at Tobias. "They want to see Dinah. They've talked to a local lawyer and one back home. That's all I know. We need to get word to the Bawells and Josie."

"When do they want to meet Dinah?"

"This weekend," Jewel said. "Can you let them know? I tried to call the hat shop, but her assistant said she had taken the afternoon off. I didn't want to send this in a message from someone else."

Tobias glanced back to the workroom. "I usually ride home with Abram."

"I can drive you to the Bawell place," Jewel said. "And give you a ride back to Abram's house after."

"That is kind, but you might have to wait."

"I can do that. We're done for the day, and the ladies can handle being upstairs alone without me for a little while. I'll alert one of our on-call volunteers, too. Alisha Braxton might not mind coming to sit with her grandmother."

Tobias agreed and went to report to Abram. "I will be home soon. Don't wait supper."

"Beth will leave you a plate on the stove," Abram said. "I hope things get worked out for all of you, Tobias."

"I pray so," Tobias said.

Somehow, he'd become the go-between with the Beningtons and the Bawells. While this made him uncomfortable, how could he refuse?

Josie would need him if…if the couple took little Dinah away.

When he saw Jewel's economy car pulling up outside the furniture market, he waved to Abram. Then he hurried out and hopped inside the automobile.

"Let's go," he told Jewel.

His friend didn't waste time pulling out onto the street.

Chapter Sixteen

The ladies were leaving for the day. Chattering and hugging each other, they gathered onto buggies or headed out on foot, waving as they left the Bawell property.

Josie let out a sigh. "I'm glad everyone came, but it's hard to keep smiling and stitching when I can't focus."

Raesha nodded, unable to speak for a moment. "I was determined to keep going on with life but, honestly, the hours seemed to drag by."

"You two need to be thankful that your friends didn't ask nosy questions," Naomi retorted. "They were kind and willing to ignore the tension we all feel. If they have heard anything, they had the *gut* sense and sweet grace to remain silent on things."

"You're right, of course," Raesha replied as she busied herself with a quick supper of sliced ham and fresh vegetables from the garden. "Josiah will be home soon and I don't want to burden him with all this worry."

Josie figured her brother had burdened himself all day, worrying about what might happen next. He'd barely talked to her over the last few days. He seemed to carry a lot of guilt, too. Or maybe he wished he'd never found her and brought her here.

Gott's will, she reminded herself. The Lord God had brought them this far. He'd see them through.

When they heard a loud knock at the front door a few minutes later, Raesha's gaze met Josie's, fear evident in the frown that marred her face.

"I'll get it," Josie said, to save Raesha

from having to leave the food simmering on the stove.

She hurried to the door and opened it, thinking maybe someone forgot something from the frolic.

Tobias stood there, his eyes bright with the same shock she'd experienced all week. "Josie, I need to speak to all of you."

Josie's heart burned with fear and dread. "Drew's parents?"

He nodded, then glanced back at the car parked underneath the shade of a big oak. Jewel sat at the wheel, the windows down so she could have some air. She gave Josie a quick wave.

Dread in her soul, Josie nodded and said, "*Kumm* inside."

When Raesha saw him, she sank down onto a chair and put her hands to her face. Naomi wheeled her chair close. "*Wilkum*, Tobias. Would you like something to drink?"

"No, thank you, Naomi. Is Josiah nearby?"

They heard the back door opening. Josiah walked in. "I'm here. I saw Jewel's car out front."

"She gave me a ride," Tobias explained. "I have news from the Beningtons."

Josiah quickly washed up and then sat down beside Raesha. She grabbed his hand like a lifeline. "What news, Tobias?"

"They are still here and they've talked to lawyers here and back in Kentucky. They want to see Dinah this weekend."

The room went silent. Josie looked up at Tobias. His gaze held hers and her world seemed to tilt. "This is my fault," she said. "I should have kept away. Dinah would be mine, free and clear. No one would have found her."

Tobias shook his head. "Drew had someone locate me, Josie. And they happened to find both of us." Giving her a regretful stare, he added, "I'm the one to blame."

"Stop that nonsense," Naomi said on a gentle admonishment. "*Gott* brought you both here for a reason. Dinah needed you, Josie, and she needs us. Tobias wanted to find you and he has. This is not over until *Gott*'s will shall prevail."

Raesha stood, her hands pressing against the heavy wood of the dining table. "Does *Gott* want us to suffer when we watch them take her away from us? They are strangers who had a horrible son. He's dying now, so they want a replacement for him."

Naomi looked surprised, but her expression filled with compassion. "They also want our forgiveness."

Josiah stood and took his wife into his arms. "It will be all right. I'll make it right, somehow."

Josie couldn't look away from Tobias. His discomfort bristled off every pore. He did not want to be here. Maybe he didn't want to be around her at all. She was damaged, ruined, a shame to her family and friends.

"You don't have to do this," she said to him. "You have no part in this. Tell the Beningtons they can speak to me directly if they want to see our Dinah."

Tobias looked shocked, his cheeks reddening as if she'd slapped him. "I do not mind, Josie. I know the truth now, and that is all I ever wanted."

Josie advanced, her frustrations boiling over. "Now you know, Tobias. Now you see what happens when I'm involved. I tried to hide this from everyone and I almost lost Dinah and myself. I was better, healing, growing. But Drew had to do one last deed to destroy me. He might say he's sorry, but he had to know what his parents coming here would do to all of us. Especially you. He wanted you to know and he wanted this to happen."

She froze, her hands going to her mouth. The hurt she saw in Tobias's eyes almost did her in. But she couldn't be the one to bring him comfort.

"Josie?" he said, his plea a whisper. "Listen to me, please."

"Neh," she replied, lifting a hand toward him. "I have to get out of here. I can't breathe. I can't go through this again."

She turned and ran out of the room,

tears brimming over. She'd hurt him yet again, and that was the last thing she'd wanted to do.

She needed air, needed to calm the nerves that jangled like chains across her body.

Why did her shame always win out? Why couldn't she just forgive herself and fight for the child she had to admit she loved? The child she had come to love too late.

Tobias couldn't move. He stared at the door that had just slammed behind Josie. Then he looked at Naomi. "What should I do?"

Naomi sat silent for a moment. "You should go and find her. Don't question her. Just stay with her, Tobias. She needs to know someone will stay with her."

He didn't question that.

He took off through the house and went out into the growing dusk, the sunset drenching the coming night in a rich burnished red streaked with shades of pink.

Where had she gone?

He looked toward the old place and saw a slight figure running across the foot-bridge. Tobias took off after her, thinking Jewel would be worried. But Jewel would understand.

He tore through the meadow, the scents of spring wafting out in sweet floral winds. The world looked etched in beauty and the woman running away from him seemed like someone in a dream.

His dream. His Josie, running from what she couldn't accept.

He had to make her see that this was not her fault. Back then, he had acted out and shown off, tried to impress her with his *Englisch* friends. And he had failed her.

How will I ever make her see?

He stopped to catch his breath and spotted her on the front porch of her old home. She seemed to always run back here when she was afraid.

Running back to the one place that had always scared her in the worst kind of way.

Josiah had found her at the Fisher place

the last time she'd run away. She'd come and found Tobias at her old home when she'd first confronted him. Now she'd gone back to the house that stood like a constant reminder of her sins and her guilt. Did she think she was unworthy of running toward anyone or anything, that she had to come back to the place that tormented her to absolve herself?

Maybe if he stayed with her and sat silent, she'd see that he had enough forgiveness and strength to cover both of their sins.

With *Gott*'s grace and will, they had to find a way back to each other.

Josie sat huddled against the corner of the porch, her breathing shallower now. This had always been her safe spot on the bad days. She'd hide here and then scoot underneath the wide railings to run away into the yard and hide in the barn or inside her favorite cluster of trees and saplings.

Now she sat, her knees pulled up and her arms wrapped tightly against her legs, the memories that had hovered like vultures circling now, returning with a force that left her stunned and speechless.

When she heard footsteps on the old planks, the panic almost returned. But she knew the person coming to find her would not physically harm her.

No, he just held her heart captive in a sweet, torturous way that brought a piercing joy and a cruel, even more piercing pain.

Tobias came around the corner in a slow stroll and stopped when he spotted her there. Without saying a word, he sat down beside her. Without saying a word, he breathed along with her as the night settled over them like a warm cloak while the sun slipped away to be replaced with a thousand stars and a half-moon that shimmer like a beacon.

After a while, he reached out his hand and wiped at her tears. Then he touched his hand to hers. He didn't force her to move or to let go of herself.

Tobias leaned against the wall, inches

from her. His knees folded up like hers, his hand warm over hers. His fingers settled against her own in a way that offered protection and peace and a safe place.

Josie sat still and quiet, her tears a silent stream of overflowing agony.

She ached to be held, to be touched, to be loved. Ached to hold Dinah again and to see her brother and Raesha smiling and laughing with their *kinder*.

The unbearable pain crested inside her, and when she thought she would drown in it, Tobias moved closer and gently pried her hands away, his fingers wrapping around hers in a soft, strong grip.

"Josie," he said. "Josie."

She let go and turned toward him, falling into his arms and holding tight as he surrounded her, his arms pulling her close, his broad shoulders offering her a place to lay her head, his presence covering her in such a safe comfort she thought she might die from the sheer beauty of it.

"It will be all right," he whispered. "I

am here and I will not let anyone hurt you ever again."

Josie heard his promise, so she held to him with all her might, thinking this was the first time she'd felt safe since the night Drew had ruined her life.

She didn't speak. There was no need. Tobias provided the quiet comfort and security she remembered so well. She loved the scent of him—the smell of pine and cedar and soap. She loved the way his steady breath calmed her and settled her.

She loved this.

But she didn't know how long this could last.

So even though this felt right, Josie couldn't let go completely. Something else would come along and destroy her all over again. It always did, didn't it?

Tobias finally spoke again after a quiet silence. "I am so sorry, Josie. So sorry for what I caused."

She lifted up to stare at him. "Why would you be sorry?"

"It is my fault," he said. "I took you to

Drew's house that night, and I wandered off and left you alone. He took advantage of that and he…took advantage of you in a way that can never be forgotten. Or forgiven."

He held her away, his eyes full of grief and regret.

"I understand why you didn't want me back in your life. I remind you of that night when I wasn't there to stop Drew. I understand why you can't love me anymore. I will respect that and leave you be, but I'm not going anywhere, Josie. I'll be right here waiting, if you can ever forgive me."

Then he stood and helped her up.

Shocked and confused, she shook her head. "Tobias, I—"

"*Neh*, don't explain. I get it now." He glanced over at the Bawell house. The lamps had been lit and shimmered through the windows, the glow of a family reaching out into the dark night.

"I should get you home. I'm sure Jewel is wondering what happened to me."

Josie couldn't speak. He thought she didn't want him because this was his fault? How wrong could a man be?

How could she show him differently when she'd pushed him away and ignored the truth and the lies between them? She'd also ignored what had been glaring at her the whole time. Tobias was a good man and she loved him. She'd fought so hard against loving him that she'd almost forgotten she was allowed to feel what her heart couldn't hide. Now it might be too late for them.

But this was Tobias. He'd absorb the blame to take the weight off of her even when he hadn't been to blame. He had been nearby and unaware that night, true. But that didn't make this his fault. Had she secretly been harboring blame for him because he'd stepped away from her?

Neh. Drew had made her believe Tobias was looking for her that night.

Tobias had had no way of knowing that. And yet now he blamed himself.

Josie didn't argue with him. Instead, she

said a silent prayer for guidance and help. And she promised herself she'd win him back and make him see that he had done nothing wrong.

Tobias had done everything right. Somehow she had to convince him of that. But with everything between them, she had no idea how she could possibly make him see reason.

Chapter Seventeen

~❧~

When they got back to the house, Tobias found Jewel eating supper with Josiah, Raesha and Naomi. Dinah was sitting in Jewel's lap, tugging at the elaborate charms on Jewel's heavy necklace. Baby Daniel cooed from his high chair.

Jewel looked up with a smile when he guided Josie back through the door. Josie had remained quiet on the short walk back, so he took that to mean she'd accepted what he'd told her.

He took full blame and now he understood that she blamed him, too. Deep down inside, she had to feel that way or she would have disputed him. When he'd held her there on the porch, he'd hoped they had broken through to each other. But not yet, he feared.

Her unspoken anger shouted at him in a loud and clear message.

"Hi," Jewel said in her upbeat way. "Dinah and I are discussing jewelry. I told her that's how I got my name. My mama loved her jewels, so when she finally had a girl after four boys, that's what she named me. Clever, huh?"

Dinah giggled with glee as Jewel bounced her and tickled her. "I know you Amish gals don't wear jewelry, but I have to confess I have a thing for it."

Josie stood off to the side, a slight smile on her face. But her eyes were misty and burning with tears.

Tobias looked around. "I'm sorry. Jewel, we should go. You'll have to drive across town in the dark."

Jewel waved a hand in dismissal. "Nope. Not yet. Dinah and I are going into her room to read a book. She gets to pick which one. But you are to sit and eat and… talk."

Giving Tobias one of her mock-stern glares, she said, "Besides, I drove all over Chicago and Philly, young man. I think I can get you across the big bridge to Abram and Beth's place."

Raesha motioned to two chairs. "You need to eat and we need to finish talking."

Josie nodded and went to wash her hands. Tobias did the same. He didn't have much of an appetite, but at least he'd be in the same room with Josie.

That brought him some comfort.

After Jewel had made a production of taking Dinah away so they could have some privacy, Josiah let Raesha get Daniel settled in his crib while he sat and watched them nibble their ham and vegetables.

When Raesha came back and sat down, he leaned forward. "We will let Drew's parents see Dinah on Sunday afternoon, with Alisha present as our lawyer. But we will fight to the finish to keep her with us. Always."

Josie finally spoke. "I am her mother. I didn't give her up. I gave her to you to raise Amish so I could be close to her."

Tobias grew hopeful. "That should be enough to convince any judge since Drew refused to sign any papers."

"Unless that judge is friends with powerful people," Josiah pointed out. "But let's hope that nothing can change for Dinah. We adopted her, and from what Alisha tells us, if Drew refused to acknowledge the child, then his parents have no legal right to raise her."

"But what if he now wants to acknowledge her as his, before he dies?" Tobias asked.

"Would he do that?" Raesha's hope deflated as she put her elbows on the table. "For sure he wouldn't do that."

Naomi lifted her hand. "We can only be sure of one thing. That the Lord God will see us through, no matter."

Tobias wondered about that, but he knew

he had to keep the faith. He prayed that this had been the plan all along, and he hoped the Lord would give them the outcome they so desired. Why should Dinah be snatched away from a family that obviously loved and provided for the child?

How could that happen, especially now that he and Josie had found each other again? Somehow they had to keep Dinah here.

Because if the child had to go away, Josie would never recover and he'd never have the opportunity to show her how much he loved her.

A little while later Jewel came out of the big bedroom on the main floor. "Dinah is fast asleep. I tell you, that is the sweetest child ever." When she saw their drooping expressions, she gently clapped her hands. "Now, we are not having any of this. You all know how this works—the Lord provides. God is good, all the time. We pray without ceasing." Winking at Josie, she said, "Did I leave anything out?"

Josiah actually smiled. "Jewel, for sure you could quote the whole Bible, ain't so?"

"So very so," Jewel replied, grinning. "Now I thank you for the food and I'm gonna take Tobias home 'cause he looks pure bushed." Putting her hands on her ample hips, she added, "We got all day tomorrow to worry ourselves."

Tobias had to agree with the woman. They wouldn't stop worrying, but they had to bide their time.

He had to bide his time and hope *Gott*'s plan would also be the plan Tobias had himself. He wanted to marry Josie. But he had to start all over proving he was worthy of that.

She'd need someone to hold her if Dinah had to go away.

Josie sat with Katy on the breezeway steps that Sunday afternoon, her hands twisting the material of her apron. "I don't think I can do this."

Katy touched a hand to her arm. "That is why I'm here. To be with you when they arrive. Nothing to be afraid of. They only want to see their granddaughter. Maybe they'll visit and then leave."

Glad she had someone to confide in, Josie stared at the sunflower fence where tender buds were popping out of the ground. "Or maybe they'll be even more determined to take Dinah away from us."

"You have the law on your side," Katy reminded her. "The law and the Lord. All the fancy lawyers in the world can't change that."

"But Alisha says they could turn the tables, make me look like a bad mother for abandoning my child." She tugged at her bonnet strings. "I am a bad mother. I am. I didn't love her enough to fight for her, but now I'd do anything to keep her near me."

"You made a huge sacrifice, Josie. You let your *bruder* and Raesha take her. It is for the best. You get to watch her grow up, and maybe one day you can explain all of this."

Josie would never be able to explain to Dinah what she'd done. "I will not break her heart," she whispered. "I will keep her close and watch her and pray she has the best life—a happy home, a *gut* husband, many children and people to love her."

"Just as you have now that you're home," Katy replied. "If you add Tobias to that, you could almost be happy."

Almost happy. "Is that as close as I'll get?"

"If you let yourself, you could be completely happy," her friend said with a soft smile. "Stop fighting that."

Josie wiped at her eyes. "I want to tell Tobias that I still love him, but now he is blaming himself for what happened. He thinks he should have been there to protect me. I can't find the words to tell him that he is wrong."

Katy shook her head, causing one of her golden curls to fall across her face. "You two need to find a spot and talk to each other, Josie. Honesty always wins out. Confession is good for that very reason."

Josie glanced over at the house where she'd sat with Tobias the other night. "We can't seem to take the next step. He was so kind to me the night we heard that Drew's parents wanted to visit Dinah. He held me and let me cry. He didn't ask a lot of questions."

"I give him high marks for that," Katy replied. "He is willing to forgive you. You have to forgive yourself."

"It is very hard," Josie admitted. "Maybe I should go for a walk while the Beningtons visit with Dinah."

"Be strong," Katy said. "Face them."

"When did you get so smart?" Josie asked, standing to stretch. The warmth of the sun shone brightly on her sunflower buds. Lifting her face, she reveled in the warmth of the afternoon. "I must go in."

"I'll take Daniel over to the *grossmammi haus*," Katy said. "If you need to leave, *kumm* and find us, *ja*?"

"I will." Josie gave her friend a quick hug. "*Denke*, Katy."

When they heard two vehicles moving up the long drive, Katy hurried to take Daniel. Josie followed, nerves making her breathing shallow. When she entered the living room, she was surprised to see Tobias coming in with Alisha.

He nodded to her and kept his gaze down. Josie could see the hurt and tension twisting his expression, the anxiety in the way he tugged at his suspenders. He stood with Alisha, waiting.

Then Theodore and Pamela Benington entered the house, causing Tobias to gaze at Josie, an unspoken message in his eyes.

Raesha pointed to the sofa while Josiah stood silent. "Please *kumm*."

"Thank you," Alisha said. Today she wore her hair up and had on a long floral skirt and a lightweight cotton blouse. Since her grandmother and her husband had both once been Amish, Alisha always respected the Amish ways. "We won't stay long."

Pamela looked uncomfortable. She sat straight up, her summer sweater a dark navy that matched her plaid pants. She clutched a triple strand of pearls. "This is very difficult," she finally said, her voice low. "Where is Dinah?"

"I'll go and get her," Raesha said. "She should be up from her nap by now."

Theodore studied the sparse room, then let his gaze settle on Josie. "I'm sorry we didn't believe you the night you came to us for help. We should have listened and we could have easily had a paternity test done once the child was born. If you'd stayed."

Josiah held up a hand. "We agreed to let you see Dinah. I did not agree to let you remind my sister of what has transpired. No changing that now. This is where we are today. Dinah has to be our first consideration."

Alisha nodded, indicating she agreed. "So, Mr. and Mrs. Benington, you can visit with Dinah today. But Josiah and Raesha followed the Pennsylvania adoption laws to the letter. The Amish take in their own, so they didn't have to officially adopt Dinah, but they wanted the protection of abiding by the state law. Josie knew what she wanted for Dinah. She wanted her to be raised Amish."

Pamela looked around. "But why? We have so much more to offer her. She'd have everything she needs—a complete education, college later and a home that is comfortable and safe."

"Our home is comfortable and safe," Josiah replied, his tone soft. "And our scholars are educated. Dinah will be happy here. Happy and Amish, as her mother wants."

"You mean, the mother who gave her up," Theodore said, glaring at Josie.

Alisha shook her head. "That will not help the situation."

Tobias stood. "Stop this. I will not allow you to judge Josie when your son is the one to blame. Him and...me. I am to blame for not watching after her."

Raesha came back in with Dinah then, so he sat down. Josie glanced over at him and saw the anger and shame in his expression. His skin blushed a burning red and his eyes flashed fire. He looked up at her and held her gaze for a moment, anguish dark in his eyes before he looked away.

Raesha must have sensed the tension. She sat down beside Josiah and forced a cheery smile. "Here is our Dinah. She is a little over two years old now."

Dinah giggled and held up two fingers and made a sound. "Tuw."

"Yes, you are learning your numbers already," Raesha replied, her smile serene while she gave the couple sitting there a stern glare.

The Beningtons completely missed the pointed remark. They were captivated by Dinah. As they glanced from her to each other, Josie saw the pain and joy merging on their startled faces. Dinah smiled at them, her dimples running deep, her blue-green eyes wide and full of innocence.

Josie wanted to run, but Tobias somehow managed to move closer to her, finding a chair to pull up beside her. She could almost feel the heat radiating from the rage she saw in his eyes. Who was he angry with? The Beningtons and Drew? Himself? Or her?

She supposed all of the above.

Chapter Eighteen

Dinah took over, pushing out of Raesha's lap to be let down. She toddled here and there, her curious gaze moving over everyone in the room. She had their rapt attention, so she took her time staring at each of them and making adorable faces, jabbering away before rushing up to Josie, her little arms reaching. "JoJo, take."

Josie inhaled a shaky breath and lifted the child up. "Hello, you," she managed to mumble. Touching a hand to Dinah's soft chestnut curls, she sat silent, too overcome to speak.

Tobias poked at Dinah's tummy, causing

her to laugh and squirm. Then he reached inside his pocket and brought out a little wooden toy—a small birdhouse with a tiny bird perched in the opening. "Here you go," he said, his voice soft now.

Josie smiled at the carved birdhouse, her heart blossoming with thankfulness. It was big enough that Dinah couldn't put any small parts in her mouth, and it looked as if he'd carved it from one piece of wood.

"That's very kind of you," she said to Tobias.

Dinah laughed and held up her prize. "Birdie."

Josiah looked as if he might burst into tears. Raesha wiped at her eyes. Naomi rolled her chair up close, her quiet strength filling the room. "Dinah, what have you? *Kumm* and show Mammi."

Dinah pushed off Josie's lap, her light green dress billowing out around her chubby legs while her bare feet hit the floor. Her light *kapp* barely contained her thick curls, but she hurried toward where

Naomi had stopped her chair near Theodore and Pamela.

That put Dinah between Naomi and the couple. Naomi lifted her arm and turned Dinah around. "Dinah, this is Theodore and Pamela. They came to visit you. Why don't you show them the gift Tobias brought to you?"

Dinah giggled and pointed to where Tobias sat near Josie. "ToTo and JoJo."

Everyone laughed at that. "You are so smart," Naomi said, smiling at the *kinder*. "'ToTo and JoJo' has a nice ring, ain't so?"

Dinah bobbed her head, her curls bouncing.

Tobias gave Josie a quick glance and looked down at his hands. Josie thought that did have a nice ring, but would it ever happen?

Pamela wiped at her eyes. "Dinah, hi. I'm…so glad to meet you. I'm Pamela. Pam."

Dinah offered her prize to Pamela to look at, then twisted around, her bare feet pressed together on the wooden floor while she turned shy.

"That's so pretty," Pamela said, glancing at Tobias before she handed the carving back to Dinah. "Did you carve this?"

"Ja," he said, looking sheepish.

Pamela's smile was bittersweet. "I still have the little car you carved for Drew. He kept it on a shelf in his bedroom."

Tobias only nodded and then shot Josie an apologetic glimpse. He was caught between the friend he'd once had and the woman who'd left him. Her heart couldn't deny empathy for him.

Theodore cleared his throat. "She looks like—"

He stopped and rubbed a hand down his face. "This is harder than I thought it would be." Glancing toward his wife, he said in a low voice, "So like him."

Pamela could only nod. "So precious and beautiful." She sniffed and touched a hand to Dinah's curls. "I can't thank you enough for letting us visit. I understand now how you must feel, thinking we'd...

do anything to upset her." Leaning down, she reached out her hands. "Dinah, would you like to sit in my lap?"

Dinah glanced at Josiah and Raesha, as if unsure.

Josiah swallowed and sighed. "It's all right, *bobbeli*. Go ahead and sit with the nice lady."

Raesha stood. "I have iced tea and cinnamon crumb cake. I'll get it ready."

Glad for something to do, Alisha did the same. "I'll pass out the tea."

"I'll help," Josie offered, but Tobias tugged at her arm, shaking his head slightly. "I'll do it."

She didn't argue with him or Alisha. He might need to move about to purge some of his anger and regret. He was usually calm when she was a mess, but today he had jumped to her defense, his own emotions spilling over.

In spite of her flaws, Tobias saw her heart. Josie could keep that realization close, at least.

She saw his heart, too, in the little carving he'd made for Dinah. The child was at no fault. Tobias knew that and accepted Dinah the way they all had. The way she now did. Had she accepted the child too late to keep her close?

Tobias had stayed close to Josie once he'd found her again. Was that how *Gott* did it? Did He remain close even when someone couldn't accept His love? Josie wished she'd been more devout in knowing the Lord watched out for His lost sheep. She could see that now. Tobias was a strong example of such a stance.

Tobias would always be the kind of man who put *Gott* and his faith first. Who looked after others with an unyielding sacrifice and stood up for what was right. She didn't deserve him and yet he was here, and he was standing by her and the child who had come between them. That same child who now held a room full of tense, worried people in the palm of her little hand.

Why had Josie held back from truly loving her daughter? She had always loved

Dinah, and she'd resented her, too. Josie had brought Dinah here out of sheer desperation and she'd returned here for the same reason—they had nowhere else to go.

Glancing around while Dinah made these sad people smile and laugh, Josie remembered Katy's words about being almost happy.

She could be completely happy if she only looked at the blessings here right in front of her.

Now she had to show Tobias he could do the same. Could they be happy here together again? No matter what?

Tobias helped Raesha serve the tea and cake while Dinah made everyone laugh with her toddler antics. She chirped like a bird, galloped like a horse and lifted her arms like a butterfly. All the noise woke Daniel, and now he was laughing and crawling behind her. Dinah had never been a fussy baby unless she was sick, but today she seemed to have picked up on the stress in the adults and had decided she'd make them feel better.

Smart child. It had worked to break the ice that gripped all of them.

After about an hour where Dinah moved from lap to lap, Alisha came up to where Josie stood by the kitchen sink. Placing her empty glass down, she turned to Josie. "Josie, you've handled yourself well today. I can only imagine how hard this has been for you."

Josie kept washing dishes, her gaze on the green fields and valleys beyond the house. "I've been through a lot, but I know this is where I belong now."

"And what about Tobias?"

Josie looked at her *Englisch* friend. Alisha had almost gotten killed over a year ago at Christmas. But Nathan had helped save her and they'd found each other again after many years apart.

Instead of answering the question, she asked one of her own. "Are you and Nathan happy now that you're back in Campton Creek and married?" she asked, curious.

Alisha's soft smile said it all. "Yes, we are. We're going to build a new house not far from our cabin, and we already have our offices set up around the corner from Campton House."

Shrugging, she said, "I never dreamed I would come back here to practice law. But Nathan loves his work, and now I love mine even more. We like the simple life here." She touched her stomach. "And... we're expanding."

"Expanding?" Confused, Josie looked down and then back at Alisha. "You're *ime familye weg*? Pregnant?"

Alisha bobbed her head, her eyes misting. "Only Nathan and a few other people know, but I'm telling you to give you hope, Josie. Nathan and I found each other again, against all the odds." She glanced at where Tobias was playing on the floor with Daniel and Dinah. "I hope you and Tobias can do the same."

Josie gave Alisha a quick hug and turned to watch Tobias with the *kinder*. "He would be a *gut daed*."

"And you are a good mother," Alisha said. "Now, I need to get them back. They're leaving tonight to go back to Drew. He's toward the last days now."

Josie thought she should feel something for Drew, some sympathy or regret. But she only felt pity for the man who had abused several young girls like her. Her only prayer for now was that his parents wouldn't take Dinah from them.

Walking over to where the Beningtons walked toward the door with Josiah and Raesha, Josie stood next to Tobias, who now held Dinah in his arms. He saw Josie and gave her a soft smile.

"Thank you again," Pamela said, her expression more serene now. "We have to get back to our son. I know the Amish don't allow for pictures, but—"

Alisha looked at Josie and then at Raesha. "Drew would like to see a picture of her."

Josie gulped in air, wishing she could make them all go away, but Tobias took her hand, grounding her.

Josiah glanced at Raesha and then Naomi. Naomi nodded. "We all have little treasures that carry us through the day. I believe one picture should be allowed."

Alisha turned to the Beningtons. "This is not to be shared with anyone except Drew. I know you'll respect that because we all want to protect Dinah's privacy."

"We will," Theodore said, his tone humble now. "We will cherish a picture of Dinah forever."

Josie felt hope stirring in her soul. That statement sounded so final and full of resolve. Had they seen that this was the right place for Dinah?

Raesha sat Dinah in her little rocking chair and chatted with her, out of the way of the phone camera, while Alisha took two quick pictures with Pamela's phone and then handed it back.

Pamela pulled up the pictures. "Perfect." She turned to Josie. "I know you don't think Drew is sorry, but he is and he really did send us here. He wants you and Tobias to be happy." She looked at the picture of Dinah. "And this will make him happy."

Tobias never let go of Josie's hand, even when she wanted to scream and wail in pain for her child and her family. She didn't do that and she didn't run away.

Instead, she straightened her spine and said, "Dinah is dear to all of us. We love her. I hope you will consider that when you talk to Drew."

Alisha gave the Beningtons a moment to speak. When they said nothing, she glanced at Josiah and Raesha. "I'll be in touch."

Pamela turned one last time. "Thank you again for letting us see Dinah." She touched a hand to Dinah's. "You are precious."

Dinah grinned and then dropped her head against Josiah's shirt. Obviously, the child was tired. Josie rushed to take her.

"I'll get her tidied up."

Josie and Tobias held back with Naomi and Dinah when the others walked outside. After they were alone with Mammi, and Dinah was down on the floor with Daniel again, Josie put a hand to her mouth and turned to Tobias. He tugged her into his arms.

"I've got you. Always," he said, his arms holding her close. "I've got you."

Dinah looked up from her toys and pointed. "ToTo and JoJo. *Ja*."

"*Ja*," Naomi echoed, clapping her hands. "You are a wise one, my little Dinah."

Tobias helped Josie finish up, and together they got Daniel and Dinah washed up and ready for dinner. Dinah was a sweet child with an open heart. Daniel gurgled and cooed, his smile as bright as his *mamm*'s. Tobias wondered what it would be like to hold a child of his own. A bitterness grabbed at his chest. Drew had forced himself on Josie. She'd had a child—without Tobias.

Because Tobias had been too addled to see the truth in front of him. Drew was no friend of his.

When Tobias caught Josie watching him

while he admired the *kinder*, he straightened up and mentally shook himself. He shouldn't be daydreaming about children, and he had to let go of the piercing bitterness that clouded his vision.

"I should go," he said, glancing at the sun. "It will be dark soon."

Naomi heard him. "Tobias, why don't you stay for supper? You've been so kind in helping us through this. Surely we can feed you."

Tobias couldn't be sure how to answer, so he deferred to Josie. Telling himself he should get out of here, he heard the words come out of his mouth. "Would you mind?"

Josie sent Naomi a firm glance. But she turned back to him. "You are *wilkum* to stay, of course. We're having sandwiches and potato salad. Not much, but none of us has much of an appetite anyway."

Tobias had been too nervous to eat much at breakfast and his stomach was protesting. "Sounds like a feast to me."

Josiah and Raesha came back inside.

"That was difficult," her brother said, running a hand down his beard. "Josie, how are you holding up?"

Josie glanced at her brother. Dark circles lined his eyes and he looked as exhausted as she felt. "I'm all right, *bruder.* I made it through, at least."

Raesha sank down on a chair. "I'll get the sandwiches out after I catch my breath. That was the hardest two hours I've ever sat through."

"We all need a little rest," Naomi said. "What do you think, Josiah? Did we convince them to leave Dinah be?"

Josiah shook his head. "I do not know. I pray so." He glanced about and said, "I'm going to check on the animals and close up the barn for the night."

He walked out before anyone could comment. Raesha sent Naomi a concerned frown, her eyes full of torment. "I don't like seeing him in this way. What should I do?"

Naomi adjusted her chair. "Let him go.

Men tend to hold things inside, but he knows you will listen when he needs you."

She gave Tobias a pointed nod. "Tobias, what about you?"

Surprised, Tobias blushed under that matronly scrutiny. "I am here because... because I hold the guilt for all of this."

He couldn't finish. He turned and went out the door, too. But instead of heading to the barn, Tobias took off toward the footbridge and then stalked to the Fisher house.

Naomi was right. Men did hold things inside, and right now he was about to explode with anger and grief for what might have been. He didn't know if he had the heart to get past any of this.

Chapter Nineteen

Josie didn't stop to think. She dropped what she'd been about to do and took off after Tobias. Knowing where he'd probably gone, she squinted in the late-afternoon sun and saw a lone figure over on the porch of the Fisher house.

Why did he always go back to that place?

Why had she been doing the same lately?

Were their memories so tied up in tangles that they both needed to go to that house for different reasons?

She made her way slowly through the tall grasses and skinny saplings that lined the old arched bridge. People around here loved bridges of all sizes and shapes. The solid structures brought everyone together and made winters lovely and summers pleasant. This small one had worked to bring her and Tobias together several times.

Was God leading her toward the path home?

Tobias lifted his head when he heard her coming, though he didn't wave or invite her up onto the porch. Well, it wasn't his house now, was it?

"Tobias," she said, her sneakers hitting the old planked porch floor. He barely looked around.

Josie decided she'd had enough of missing out on her dreams. She'd win him back, completely. Somehow. It wasn't lost on her that she'd fought him with every fiber of her being, and even still she didn't feel worthy of him. But her heart skipped right over those important details. Having him near today had helped her through dealing with Drew's parents.

But, right now, Tobias didn't want to

hear her words of encouragement and appreciation.

So she didn't speak again. She scooted up beside him and stood staring out at the view. This was the best spot on the property to see the fields and valleys and the bridges that took people back and forth to Campton Creek.

Crops waved green and shiny new across the fields. The clean lines of earth formed a sweet symmetry that lifted and shifted over the valley, the highs and the lows merging against the golden shots of sunshine. Off in the distance, wildflowers popped here and there, lending color amid the fresh green and the brown earth.

"This is a beautiful spot," Tobias finally said. "I'd planned to talk to Josiah again about buying it, but now I don't know. Maybe it is a bad idea, considering."

She didn't speak for a moment. She had to adjust her mindset with the image of him previously wanting to live here and now suddenly wondering if he shouldn't.

Her heart burning, she asked, "Have you

changed your mind, then? Because of all that you now know about me?"

He turned to her, his eyes going dark with understanding. "Josie, no, no. I didn't mean because of you. You are not at fault. I feel responsible for what happened to you, so I can now see why you pushed me away."

Did he think that? All this time he'd been here, she had pushed him away, but not because she blamed him. Although if she'd been honest, she did feel angry at him for taking her to Drew's house that night. Had she been subconsciously holding that against Tobias?

He glanced over at her, apprehension in his eyes. His expression went to stone. "You do blame me. You still don't want me to stay in Campton Creek, do you?"

They stood looking into each other's eyes, so many unspoken words between them. Everything went quiet and still, the trees calming. Even the birds seemed to settle and wait.

Finally, Josie gave in to what her heart

already knew. "I think buying this farm is a fine idea, Tobias. You should stay here. You have a job and you have found a place to make your own. I don't have any right to stop you."

He finally pivoted to face her, the agony etched on his face now turning to relief and hope. "Are you certain sure?"

Josie wasn't sure of anything right now, but her heart seemed to know better than her mind. "I am certain sure."

He let out a breath. "*Gut,* because I gave your *bruder* a good-faith payment to hold it for me, and time is running out."

"You did what?" she asked, her head fuzzy with confusion. "You mean, all this time, Josiah and you cooked up a deal, thinking I'd finally cave?"

Tobias had the good grace to blush. "No. It's not like that."

"It sounds like that," she retorted, trying to decide if she should be extremely mad or very glad. The old, misguided Josie would have lashed out. Today, after everything they'd had to deal with, she couldn't muster up any anger toward her brother or this man. But she was a bit confused. "My own kin, lying to me."

"He did not lie. He withheld a business transaction."

Josie finally smiled, able to accept that she wasn't all that mad after all. "I will deal with Josiah when I get back home. Are you still staying for supper?"

"Am I still invited for supper?"

"Ja," she said, liking this new easiness surrounding them. But she knew the underlying problems were still there. *"Ja,* I think we should all stick together right now. Josiah will need a friend and…we all need you."

His expression changed and softened with relief. "Josie, do *you* need me?"

She wouldn't lie to him ever again. "I think I do, but I'm afraid. I need you to be patient with me, Tobias. I know it's asking a lot because you've already been through a lot. I left you, I wasn't honest with you, I pushed you away, and now you know the worst there is to know about me. And yet you're still here. I just need you to be patient."

"Josie," he said, taking her into his arms. "I am a very patient man. I'll talk to Josiah and get this house sale settled. Then I'm going to fill this place, piece by piece, with beautiful things so that if you do decide to move in here one day, you won't have any bad memories at all. I only want you to have good memories."

Josie's heart beat too fast. "What if I can't let go of those horrible memories? I have not had the best life and a lot of that was my doing."

"No, most of that was others doing things to hurt you. I am not one of those others. I'm Tobias. Your ToTo. The man who never forgot you. I'll be here, no matter what."

He tugged her into his arms and held her close. "I have missed you, Josie."

Josie allowed this small comfort. Tobias wouldn't leave her and he would never hurt her. He would wait for her. She had to cling to that.

Then she lifted up to stare at him. "You are not to blame, so don't go thinking that about yourself. I came out here to tell you that. I want you to understand."

Tobias looked bashful and unsure again. "I feel responsible, Josie. I was trying to be someone I could never be, and I left you while I trudged around that big house with Drew's friends. When I look back on it, I'm ashamed that they probably knew what was going on and lured me away. And I fell for that because my pride wanted to believe I was somebody important to them."

Seeing the raw torment in his eyes, Josie touched a hand to his face. "We have both changed and now we see the clear path. But we don't have to rush anymore, Tobias. We start over, in a million little ways."

His torment changed to mirth. "Now you sound like Bettye. She told me that is how I should win you back—with a million little ways."

Amazed, Josie took his hand and tugged

him toward supper. "So you sent flowers and carved me the butterfly, and then our worlds fell apart again when Drew's parents showed up."

"*Ja*, but I have a lot of little things left to make you forgive me and…come back to me."

Josie shook her head. "That could take a while." Then she amended, "There is nothing to forgive, Tobias. But I have to be sure. I've been hiding here so long, isolated and in fear, I'm not sure I can be the girl you fell in love with, ever again."

"As you said, we don't have to rush," he replied. "Except to supper. I am for sure starving."

Josie smiled at him. "This was a hard day. The worst. But you made it tolerable."

"That's why I'm here," he said, his tone and his expression turning serious. "To make up for everything that has come before."

When they got back to the house, Josiah had returned and washed up. He glanced toward them when they came in the back door. "Supper," he said, his tone almost angry.

Josie's mind whirled with a shaky antici-pation mixed with a tentative contentment. She and Tobias had reached a crossroad of sorts, although there was still so much between them. Dinah had to come first. Josie would not lose her yet again.

Raesha and Naomi gathered them around the table and Raesha passed out roast-beef sandwiches on fresh sliced bread, as well as pickles and fresh toma-toes. Naomi served the potato salad from her wheelchair. Then she poured fresh cold tea into their glasses.

"Denke," Tobias said. "For letting me stay today and for supper tonight."

"You are *wilkum* anytime," Naomi re-plied. "Now let us pray."

Everyone bowed their heads in silence.

Josie knew what her prayers held. She wanted Dinah here and safe, and she told the Lord she'd show more love than she already had to her child. She also prayed that, somehow, Drew's parents would not press the issue of taking Dinah away. Then she asked the Lord to show her the way back to Tobias, with no guilt or regrets between them, so they could have the life they'd always planned, but here, together.

And then she prayed with all of her might that she'd be able to live in the house that had shaped her and changed her and still to this day frightened her.

How could she ever make that happen?

Tobias followed Abram into the workshop the next morning, his heart lighter now that he and Josie had gotten closer. It would be a long haul to bring her completely around, but at least she was willing to allow him back into her life.

"So how did it go yesterday?" Abram asked after he'd examined a cabinet they'd been sanding. Finding a rough spot, he picked up a sanding cloth and worked on the dark wood. "It was late when we heard you return. You must have gone to bed right after."

Tobias picked up a polish rag and started going over the wood so he could stain it and bring out the beautiful grain that reminded him of a tiger's stripes.

He nodded. "It was a hard day, watching Drew's parents with little Dinah. She is a precious child, and Josiah and Raesha have done a wonderful good job of taking care of her."

"But?"

Tobias dropped his rag. "But I see Drew in her and… I resent that."

"You resent what your friend did, or you resent the child?" Abram asked, his hand stilling on the wood.

"I resent and regret all of it. I was supposed to protect Josie from such awful things and I failed."

"Let's get some of that fresh coffee I smell," Abram suggested. "At least our craftsmen know how to make *gut* coffee, ain't so?"

Tobias followed him to the corner break room and took a cup of the hot brew. He wished he'd never mentioned his feelings, but he needed to vent to someone and Abram was a wise listener and counselor.

Abram wasn't about to let up, either. "You have much on your shoulders," he said, his voice low while the other workers laughed and went about their duties. "Too much. You need to remember *Gott* has a plan for each of us."

"I tell myself that," Tobias replied. "But I get impatient with whatever the good Lord has cooked up for me. Josie and I have lost a lot of time together already."

Abram stared into his coffee as if trying to see answers there. "I do not think He's cooked up anything. His timing is perfect, even when we veer off the path. If we stay the course in our faith, He will bring us back around again."

Tobias gave him a smile. "Josie and I did reach a truce of sorts. She has agreed to me buying the Fisher place."

"Well, there you go," Abram said before draining his coffee. "See, that's a good step in the right direction."

"It is," Tobias agreed. He took a couple

of sips and then rose to get back to work. "I'm going to meet with Josiah today to get all the paperwork straight. But we are moving along."

"And Josie is okay with that, you said. So there is hope."

Tobias nodded. "She is okay with me buying the property, but we have a long way to go to get back where we were."

"If you marry, will she live in that house?"

"That's the part I'm not sure about," Tobias said, his gaze moving over the cabinet he needed to finish. The wood had started out rough and edged with splinters. Humans could be much the same. "I have to keep working on things with Josie, I think. We're polishing out the rough spots, and I hope one day, together, we'll both be healed."

"Now, that's the kind of attitude I like to hear," Abram said, slapping him gently on the back. "It will all work out for the *gut*, Tobias."

Tobias wanted to see that day. "I'd best

get this polished and stained so it can dry properly before Nancy Henderson comes back wanting to load it on her truck."

"She is persistent and she has green money," Abram said, chuckling. "The *Englisch* do have their bright spots."

After they'd both settled into their routines, Tobias thought about all the changes in his life. He was so close to having what he wanted at last—a new home and being back with Josie.

But he feared she might not ever want to live in the house he was buying. She'd asked him to be patient and he would be, but had he pushed her too much, insisting he must live in the one place she'd tried to escape? Would it be a mistake to ask her to live there with him?

In *Gott*'s time, he reminded himself.

Meantime, he'd start courting her properly again, and he'd plan out next spring's crops so he could get his farmers' market up and running. Between work here and doing that on the side, he'd be a busy man. Josie might enjoy helping with the farmers' market. He'd build a strong shed out by the road and make it comfortable enough so they could both sit there and sell fresh produce. That would be nice.

Staying busy and saving up money between now and then would be his next goal. He wanted to make sure Josie had everything she'd need to start their new home together.

But he would never be too busy to forget how much he had missed Josie and how his insides boiled with anger each time he thought of how Drew had treated her.

He'd have to send up a lot of prayers to get past that image. Before he could even form a prayer, the furniture market's front door opened and Mary Zook peeked inside.

"Tobias, you're here. I'm so glad."

Chapter Twenty

Josie finished snapping the beans she'd gathered from the garden. She and Naomi would have beans and ham with fresh sliced tomatoes tonight for their dinner. They needed some quiet time.

It had been a week since the Beningtons had visited and, while the whole family had calmed down, Josie couldn't rest. She checked on Dinah all day long and took her for walks around the property, pointing out trees and flowers along the way.

Dinah loved to chatter and she absorbed new words easily. "Tree. Pine?"

"Pine is correct," Josie proudly told her this afternoon.

"Bidge," Dinah said, her hand waving toward the arched footbridge to the Fisher place.

"Bridge," Josie replied. "Bridge."

"Bidge. Go."

They'd walked across the footbridge over and over until finally Dinah had turned toward home because she wanted a drink of water.

Home. What if Dinah lost her home and had to go to a new home far away? The thought of Dinah growing up in that huge, cold house where she'd been conceived in such a horrible way made Josie feel ill.

She didn't like having these disturbing flashbacks.

"What is wrong with you tonight?" Naomi asked. "I know you are concerned, as we all are, but I thought things were better with you and Tobias."

"Things are better," Josie said, heading to the sink to wash the beans and get them boiling in the pot. "Or at least I thought they were."

Rumors showed a different picture, however. Another thing for Josie to fret about.

"Child, come and tell me," Naomi said from her comfortable chair in the small living area.

Josie watched the water begin to boil. Then she dropped in the beans and seasoning, making sure the bits of ham she'd broken to flavor the beans covered the top.

After lowering the heat, she sat down across from Naomi. "Katy told me Mary Zook is bragging about how Tobias helped her design a side table for her mother. Apparently, she spent most of this week in and out of the shop, checking on the progress of the piece."

"I see," Naomi said with a soft smile. "Well, he is talented and he has to make money, so why does this bother you so?"

Josie stared across at Mammi, wondering what was going through her mind. "I don't mind him making furniture or money, but I do mind Mary Zook spending a lot of time with him. She's been after a husband since before I came back home."

"Oh, I see. So you don't want her to have the man who should be your husband, ain't so?"

Josie blinked and frowned at Naomi. "I didn't say that."

Naomi went back to her knitting. "No, you didn't say that at all. But your expression and the jealousy in your words told me that."

Josie got up to check the beans and slice the ham. "You are imagining things."

"I might be old and I can barely see what I'm knitting, but I know you still care deeply about Tobias."

"I will always care about him."

"So why are you worried about Mary Zook?"

Josie whirled, shame coloring her face. "Because she told Tobias she'd heard he was seeing a lot of me and then she asked him if he knew about me."

Naomi's teasing expression turned sour. "That young woman needs a good talking-to. She knows not to spread gossip."

"But it's true," Josie said. "It's true, and since I haven't heard from Tobias all week, I'm wondering if he sees how horrible it would be if he's with me."

Naomi tried to stand. "Bring me my chair."

"Neh," Josie said, thinking Naomi would make her hitch the buggy so they could go confront Mary. "I am okay. Tobias is free to talk to other people. It's just that I'll never be completely forgiven and this community will never completely forget."

Naomi settled back, her frown remaining. "You need to know that the people who count have accepted you back and you do not have anything to be ashamed of. You confessed before the church, and the bishop himself approved you living within our community. Mary Zook is just trying to stir up trouble because she is the jealous one. She knows you are loved and she knows what she's doing."

Josie was about to tell Naomi to calm herself when they heard a knock at the back door.

"That is probably my brother wondering if we're arguing. I've already had a talk with him about keeping it secret that Tobias had made a down payment on our old place."

"We never argue," Naomi said on a soft huff. "We heavily discuss. And besides, Josiah knows tonight is our alone dinner here at home. He's probably embarrassed that we found out about what he's done and he's come to apologize for keeping all of us, including his wife, in the dark."

"I'll just go and see." Josie hurried to the breezeway door and opened it wide, expecting to see Josiah or Raesha waiting.

Tobias stood there, looking uncomfortable and unsure.

Had he come to tell her he didn't want to be with her after all? His gaze shifted everywhere but on her.

"May I come in?" he asked when he finally did look at her, his eyes full of a mysterious light.

Josie glanced back at Naomi. "We're about to have supper."

"Let the man in," Naomi said with a wave of her hand. "And invite him to eat with us."

Josie moved aside, hoping Naomi wouldn't keep chattering. "Have you eaten?"

"I came straight here from work," Tobias replied. "I have my own buggy now. Abram helped me fix up an old one, and he loaned me a buggy horse he keeps in town to make deliveries."

"We are about to eat," Naomi said, hearing him. "Josie, turn down the beans and we'll fry up the ham after Tobias washes up. Take him out to the pump on the porch."

Josie took the hint and turned back toward the porch. "She can be bossy sometimes."

Tobias tried to hide the grin tugging at

his mouth. "She wants us to have alone time, which is what I need right now."

Forgetting the pump and water, Josie whirled. "You came to tell me that you've changed your mind about everything, haven't you? You've come to your senses and you don't really want me in your life anymore?"

Tobias stepped back, drawing his head away so he could see her clearly. "Whatever gave you that idea?"

"Mary Zook," she said before she could stop herself. "She's telling everyone that she and you have been spending a lot of time together. And that you should stay away from me."

Tobias started laughing.

"You think that is funny?" Josie asked, an image of him laughing with Mary making her want to run away and get out of his sight. Or maybe throw cold water on him.

"I'm laughing because I've never seen you so worked up, not since I've been here. And I've seen you a lot of ways, Josie. Sad and upset, embarrassed and afraid, but not like this. You do care about me certain sure."

"I only care that you'll fall into Mary's trap. She wants a man, Tobias. Any man."

"Oh, so she's just flirting with me because she'll take any man who comes along?"

"That's not what I meant and you know it."

He tugged her close, his hands holding hers, his eyes full of confidence and hope now. "So what do you mean?"

Josie tried to pull away. "Nothing. It's just she's gossiping about me, telling people you shouldn't be with me." Shrugging, she added, "Hearing that brings up all of the bad memories I've tried so hard to push away."

Tobias touched a hand to her cheek, his fingers rough from work but soft to the touch. His jaw muscles went tight, his eyes no longer full of teasing mirth. "This is why I came to see you. I heard what she'd said and, Josie, I set her straight about all of it."

Josie's heart went from hurting to rejoicing. "What did you tell her?"

"I told Mary Zook that I'd finished the little table she had to have for her *mamm*'s birthday and then I loaded it on her buggy for her. She gave me some freshly baked oatmeal cookies and I ate one while she smiled at me. Then I explained that I did not like people gossiping about you and that I came here because of you."

Josie took in a breath and put her hand over his on her cheek. "You said that to her?"

"*Ja*, and more." He grabbed her hand and brought it between them, putting it close to his heart. "I told her I know all about what you've been through and that I admire you even more than I did before. And then I said that one day I plan to marry you."

Josie felt his heart beating against her palm, her own pulse matching the steady rhythm. "You said all of that with a mouthful of oatmeal cookie?"

"I waited until I'd chewed that one, and I ate the second one after I'd explained things to her." He grinned, his nose touching Josie's. "She left in such a rush she almost slung that pretty little cabinet off into the gravel."

"She did not."

"She did," he said, leaning close. "I told you the truth. Mary Zook is not the woman for me, and I'm pretty sure she won't be gossiping about you ever again."

"Tobias," she said, pulling him close. "I do not deserve you."

"You're right," he replied as he leaned close. "You deserve way better than me."

She gave him a quick, shy kiss and then turned, taking him by the hand. His gaze on her told her he wanted the kiss to last longer, but someone might see them here. "Get cleaned up. I have to fry the ham."

"I'll set the table and help you," he replied. "Then your brother and I have some important business to take care of."

She whirled, her fingers on the door-knob. "You are buying the house."

He nodded. "Are you sure you want me to do that?"

"I am," she replied, her hidden fears tamped down for now. "I did give Josiah a hard time about keeping secrets from me, but he made a good point. If I'd known, I would have fought against both of you."

Tobias hurried to wash his hands and face, and grabbed a towel hanging on the hook next to the pump. "You don't have to fight anyone anymore, Josie. Remember that."

Josie wanted to remember that, but they might have one more big fight before they could finally work their way back to each other.

The Beningtons could return any day now. She was fiercely afraid of what they would demand from her family.

Chapter Twenty-One

$\sim$

Josiah smiled over at Tobias. "Looks like the Fisher farm belongs to you now, Tobias. I'll get this paperwork to Alisha Craig, and I'll take your check to the bank first thing tomorrow."

Tobias reached across the dining table to give Josiah a handshake. "A fourth up front, then monthly payments, and so on and so on, until I'll have you paid in full."

They'd discussed the plan and Josiah had agreed. Since no Realtor was involved, they could make their own rules, but Alisha had drawn up a simple contract that stated the terms of the transaction.

Now it was done.

"I know where you'll be living," Josiah replied after shaking his hand. "I'll come looking for my money if you miss a payment. But you're wise to pay on the installment plan rather than handing me the rest of your savings. Might need that for another day."

Josiah had to be referring to Josie. If they got married, Tobias wanted to have some money in the bank to get them going.

"A rainy day," Tobias replied, thinking of furniture and gardens and children. Would he and Josie have children? He hoped so.

Josiah nodded and gave Tobias a solemn glance. "Do you think Josie will live there with you?"

That was the one thing Tobias couldn't predict. "I do not know. I'd like to believe our love can overcome even the memories of that house, but I have wondered if I'm doing the right thing." Looking toward the door, he added, "She told me she wanted me to do this, but she did not say if *she* wanted this, too."

Josiah tugged at his beard. "It could be *gut* for her to start fresh there with new, happy memories. But I warn you—things need to go slow with Josie."

Tobias stared down at the typed words on the simple contract they'd agreed upon. "Or she might bolt and I'll lose her all over again."

"Ja," Josiah replied. "She did not want to return here, but...we are so glad she did."

They were alone in the kitchen of the main house. Raesha had taken Dinah and Daniel over to see Naomi and Josie while the men conducted business.

The quiet centered Tobias even as he was anxious to get on with his new life. "All I can do is hope that my love will see her through."

"Your love and the Lord's grace," Josiah replied. "Raesha and I had a lot to work through when I first returned here. Even before we realized we wanted to be together, she was willing to take Josie into her home. She did it for me and because she believed it was the right thing to do. It wasn't easy, loving Dinah and knowing her real mother would be close by. We've all worked hard to be a family, and we were doing fine."

Tobias looked down at the table. "Until I showed up, and then the Beningtons after that."

Josiah's smile was bittersweet. "You did throw a wrench into things, but I believe you are helping Josie to see that she is worthy of love. Her moods have improved now that she's accepted you being here."

"But?"

"But we always knew there was the possibility that the boy who did this might show up or try to make trouble one day. When we heard Drew had gone to prison, we all breathed a sigh of relief and Alisha did the right thing by getting in touch with him in prison on our behalf. As Alisha explained to the Beningtons in that first meeting, he immediately refused any claims on Dinah because he knew it would prove him guilty of what he'd done." Josiah shook his head. "Sometimes, I wish I'd never agreed to finding him and telling him he had a child. If we'd kept her a secret, we'd all be going on with our business and raising Dinah as we'd planned."

Tobias could see the apprehension in Josiah's eyes. "I understand that feeling. Drew committed a crime, the worst kind of assault on a woman, but now he wants to make restitution before he dies. So that means even though the law is on our side, his parents could make demands simply because they have the means and they want their grandchild with them."

"Just another wrinkle to get through," Josiah said. "So if you truly love my sister, you'll need to be strong for her. If something happens and we have to give Dinah to them, we will all be devastated, but Josie will not recover. And then we'll lose her forever."

"I'm not going anywhere," Tobias said, waving the paper. "This should prove that.

If Josie can't marry me, I will still be here, waiting for her to change her mind."

Josiah studied Tobias for a moment. "Then I wish you well with your new home, Tobias."

They shook hands again, then walked over to the *grossmammi haus* together. Josiah turned to Tobias when they reached the door. "Are you coming in to share the news?"

Tobias nodded. "I want to talk to Josie before I head back to Abram's house."

He needed to know how she really felt about this.

Josie glanced up when the men entered. While Daniel and Dinah had played with some wooden blocks, Raesha and Naomi had grilled her about Tobias buying the farm.

"I'm fine with it," she'd told them earlier. "He needs a place to live and he wants to grow produce to sell up on the road. That and working with Abram will keep him busy."

They'd chatted a while about the merits of hard work. Tobias had never been afraid of doing what needed to be done. He went after what he wanted in life, his plans solid and thought-out. Not like Josie, with just dreams and nothing solid to count on.

"And where do you fit in?" Raesha had asked, her smile serene while she kept one eye on the *kinder.*

"I don't know yet," Josie had admitted. "I am glad that Tobias knows the truth now, but we have so much to work through and many decisions to make."

The door had opened before they could continue, leaving Raesha and Naomi giving her concerned glances.

"The paperwork is complete," Tobias said with a smile, his gaze moving over Josie. "I now own the land across the footbridge."

Josie's heart did that quick jump of fear that always happened when she thought about her old home. She'd gone after Tobias the other day, but she'd been so intent on soothing him that her heart had steadied before she even realized where they were.

Then she remembered him finding her there on the porch a few days ago and holding her while she cried. Remembered how she'd run over there when Josiah had first gone to talk to Tobias about buying the place. What a broken mess she'd been that day, drenched from the rain and terrified of seeing Tobias up close.

But, looking back, she could see the pattern that linked her to the Fisher house.

After she'd been released from the hospital and had been back here for a while, afraid that she'd lose Dinah again, she'd taken Dinah to the old place to hide out. Josiah had found her in an upstairs bedroom. So much had changed since the night Josiah had found her inside the house, holding her baby close.

Sometimes she truly believed *Gott* had led her to leave Dinah with the Bawell women. This was where Dinah belonged. Josie belonged here now, too. Moving across the way would be like taking an ocean voyage.

No. The place could not be a threat to her anymore. She had to overcome her memories and her fears. Maybe she'd be able to handle all of it, after all, with Tobias by her side.

"Josie?"

She looked up to find her brother and Tobias staring at her. "What?"

"I asked if you are sure about this," Josiah said, his gaze tender.

"I will be fine," she said. "The worst is over. Tobias knows my secrets and he's still here. It will be nice having him next door."

Tobias shifted on his brogans. "Josie, can we take a walk and talk?"

She stood and looked toward Raesha and Naomi. They both inclined their heads.

Dinah had been playing with blocks in the corner, but she jumped up, teetering. "Go walk."

"Neh," Raesha said, grabbing her up to tickle her tummy. "Go bathe."

"Walk with ToTo," Dinah retorted, pointing a chubby finger at Tobias.

"Go get bath," Josiah replied with a big grin. "Like a fish." He began to make bubble sounds and pretend he was swimming.

Distracted by his antics, Dinah stopped fretting long enough for Tobias and Josie to slip out onto the porch.

The air was fresh with the gloaming, but the sun hadn't gone all the way down. A hint of coolness filled the warm dusk, its gentle wind flowing across Josie's face.

"Will you walk with me over to the house?" Tobias asked, his tone full of hope.

Josie glanced at the home she'd once lived in. This was it, then. Time for her to see if she could do this.

"Josie?"

She glanced from Tobias to the property he had just bought. The house glowed white, with a shimmering sheen of creamy sunshine covering it in the same way it had the night she'd first seen Tobias there. Looking at it now, she thought it looked new and shiny and ready for someone to make it a real home.

"Who would ever dream you'd come here and own this house," she said. "Who would ever dream we'd be standing here together."

"I dreamed it," he said, taking her hand. "I dreamed it night and day from the time you left me until now. But the dream isn't complete, is it?"

Josie's gaze moved from him to the house. Now that this was real and he was here to stay, planning to live over there, her world shifted yet again and settled back, her heart thudding and jumping. *Help me, Lord.*

Would she be able to do this? Why did the thing she'd longed for the most still seem just aside of her grasp. Could she find the strength to start a new life here with Tobias, finally?

Tobias waited her out. He'd do that. He'd wait. But would that be fair to him? To have to wait on her to decide? To have to wait on her to change? To wait on whether they'd lose Dinah or not?

"How long are you willing to do this, Tobias?"

He looked confused and defeated. "Do what?"

"Wait on me. You waited back in Kentucky and I never returned. Now you've bought this house and you'll wait for me even longer? Even if I can't set foot back inside that house? Even if we lose Dinah?"

Tobias tugged her close, his eyes washing her with the same warmth that had settled over the house. "Walk with me, Josie."

How could she resist him? He'd always been the one. She loved him with a deep, abiding love, but a love she'd held close like a secret, in the same way she held the wooden treasures he'd carved for her close to her heart each night before she went to sleep. The little horse and the beautiful butterfly. Her treasures from this man, the wood warming from her touch in the same way she felt safe and warm whenever he touched her.

He must have sensed the conflict warring in her soul. "You have to know that from now on, I will protect you, I will cover you, I will take care of you," he said, his tone soft and husky. "I wasn't there before when you needed me the most, but I am here now and I will make sure no one ever hurts you again."

She stopped him when they reached the footbridge. "And what about you, Tobias? Who will hold you and protect you? I wasn't there when you needed me, either, but I hope I can make that up to you now." Shaking her head, she looked down at her sneakers. "I do not want to hurt you again, ever."

"I hope that, too, but having you with me now makes up for you having to go away before," he said. "Look, Josie. Look at us. Here we are on the bridge between your world and mine. I want you in mine and I'm willing to wait for that to happen."

Then he leaned toward her and kissed

her, a soft touch of his lips to hers. Josie's heart sighed as she held to him, the memory of their time together coming back in a sweet flow of love and need. For a moment, the old doubts crowded in and the tormented memories tried to take over. Her shame, her pain and the realization that she'd convinced herself that she could never marry him almost stopped her in her tracks. She wanted to turn and go, but she had to stop running, didn't she?

When he pulled away, she stared into his eyes and mustered up her courage. "Why don't we go and look at the house before it gets too dark."

Tobias smiled and took her hand.

Josie held her breath, said her prayers and promised herself she would never let this man down again. Crossing this bridge with Tobias was all she'd ever wanted, and maybe it was fitting that they should want to make a home together here in this place.

Did *Gott* want this to be their home? Or were they trying to change a past that would never leave them alone or let them forget?

She stopped in the yard, the shadows coming toward her like creeping memories, her hand tight inside of Tobias's. Josie took deep breaths, smelled the scents of honeysuckle and fresh grass, of water and earth, of hope and peace, felt the last of the sun shining on her face.

She closed her eyes and breathed it all in. This moment, if she could just keep this moment.

"Josie?"

She opened her eyes and saw Tobias there. "I'll be all right. I have you back and we'll take the rest as it comes."

"You don't have to go inside tonight," he replied. "You're right. For now, this is enough."

Then he tugged her close and told her about his dreams for this place.

And for once, Josie didn't even notice the darkness.

Chapter Twenty-Two

Josie could almost relax now.

It was easy to see her future. While Tobias had not officially asked her to marry him, they were becoming closer every day. He'd been by several times to move things into the Fisher house. Now that he had a serviceable buggy, he'd bought a strong quarter horse to get him around and to help him clear the land behind the house.

Today she watched from her perch on the breezeway as Tobias and several men from the community, including her brother and Abram, helped him to haul logs from some trees they'd cut down on the back corner of the property. Abram wanted to pick the best of the hardwood, of course. The rest would be used for firewood or shredded into mulch that Mr. Hartford would sell at the general store.

Josie took a sip of her lemonade and watched as the sun began its descent toward the west. She'd worked in the hat shop most of yesterday and today. Long days, but she always enjoyed learning how to steam and press the rims and ribbons to make the straw summer hats that the Amish men wore to work. Raesha had started the seamstresses to making prayer *kapps*, too. They now made them in both white and black sturdy silk or lightweight organdy and muslin, and shipped them out on a daily basis.

If she and Tobias did marry, she hoped Raesha would let her work part-time to earn some household money.

If.

Such a tiny word for so many things in life. Raesha had sent her home while she finished up some paperwork. When Dinah had begged to come with her, Josie had put her down for a nap inside the main house and left the back door open so she could hear her. Daniel was sleeping in the tiny office behind the front desk of the hat shop.

That gave Josie a few moments to watch the men at work, their figures tiny since they were far from the Fisher house.

When she heard a car roaring up the dirt-and-gravel lane, her heart stilled, frozen against her ribs. Josie hopped up and saw the Beningtons getting out of a fancy taxi.

They were coming toward the house.

She ran inside the *grossmammi haus* to alert Naomi.

"They're back," she said, out of breath.

"Who?" Naomi asked from where she sat reading the local paper.

"Drew's parents," Josie said. "Raesha is still at the hat shop. I'll go and check on Dinah."

Naomi nodded. "Bring her here with us."

"I have to warn Raesha," Josie said, her mind reeling. They were back for a reason. They wanted Dinah.

"Where is Josiah?"

"With Tobias and the others, clearing the land out beyond the house."

Naomi glanced at the door. "He should be here."

"I'll take Dinah and try to let Raesha know they are here."

She rushed into the room where Dinah sat playing in the crib. "JoJo."

Josie picked up the child and kissed her cheek. "JoJo is here."

Then she hurried to the hat shop, surprising the seamstresses and the men working the steam machines when she entered through the back door. When she reached the door between the workroom and the front shop, she saw Pamela and Theodore through the partially opened door, already talking to Raesha.

Carefully opening the swinging door an inch, she listened.

"We just want her to see her father," Pamela was saying, tears in her eyes. "Drew would like to see her before it's too late. Please, let us have some time with her and our son together."

"You're asking me to hand over my child?" Raesha said, shaking her head. "Did your lawyers tell you to do this?"

"No," Theodore replied. "Drew asked us. We're trying to avoid lawyers."

They wanted to take Dinah to see Drew. No, that would put trauma in Dinah's mind and confuse her. No.

Raesha glanced back, probably concerned about Daniel. Josie and Dinah were hidden from sight and the hum of the work machines drowned out Dinah's chatters.

Josie didn't stop to think. She whirled and went back out the way she'd come and then took off walking as fast as she could.

She went past the *grossmammi haus* and hurried to the main house. After gathering food and clothing, she left by the front door, careful to stay out of sight, Dinah giggling as if they were on a grand adventure.

She had to keep Dinah away from Drew's parents. If they took Dinah all the way to Kentucky, she might not ever see her daughter again.

"Go walk," Dinah said, squirming to get down.

"It's all right," Josie said on a winded whisper. "I have to hold you, sweetheart."

"Walk," Dinah said on a stern demand.

They made it to the road, but she stayed near the tree line, darting from tree to tree so no one would notice them. When she reached the drive to the Fisher place, Josie stopped.

Where should she take Dinah?

The men were finishing for the day when Tobias heard someone shouting.

He turned to find Raesha rushing across the footbridge, her arms waving in the air.

"Josiah," he called, pointing.

All of the men stopped what they were doing and hurried from the copse of trees they'd been harvesting to run back toward the Fisher house.

"What's wrong?" Josiah asked as he grabbed Raesha by her arms.

"The Beningtons came again. They want to take Dinah to Kentucky to be with Drew until…until he passes. I told them I'd have to talk to you and I was worried about Josie."

"Where is she?"

Raesha gulped a breath. "I don't know. Drew's parents came around to the hat shop and we talked for a while. Then Daniel woke, and I brought him home and went to check on Josie. Naomi said she had gone to get Dinah up and had not returned."

Josiah's eyes filled with fear and concern. "What do you mean?"

"I can't find Josie and Dinah," Raesha said. "They are gone."

Tobias glanced around. They'd all been so occupied with getting these trees down they hadn't noticed anything unusual going on at the Bawell place or back at the house here. But his instincts kicked in.

Looking toward his house off in the distance, he turned to Raesha. "Gone?"

Raesha's eyes watered, tears streaming down her face. "I don't know. The Beningtons finally left, but they said they'd be back. Do you think they had someone take Dinah while they were talking to me? Maybe Josie went after them somehow?"

Josiah took Raesha into his arms. "We will find them."

Tobias tugged at his hat and searched the countryside. "Surely they wouldn't do that. Did they have a court order to take Dinah?"

Raesha shook her head. "They only wanted to know if we'd allow it and I said no. But I did tell them we would discuss this. We can't let them take her without one of us with her, if we agree to this at all."

"We won't let that happen," Josiah said. "Go back and stay with Daniel and Naomi. We will search for Dinah and Josie. I'll call Nathan, too. He'll get to the bottom of this."

Tobias turned to the other men. "We need to call it a day."

Abram nodded. "We'll help you look for the *bobbeli*. But we should hurry. The sun will go down soon."

"And Josie," Tobias replied. "I'm going to find her. I have a feeling that wherever Josie is, Dinah will be with her."

"Walk," Dinah said, her bare feet pattering on the wooden floor.

"We did walk," Josie replied, wishing she'd thought this through a little better. "But we need to get out of here, don't we?"

She'd panicked, no doubt. The first panic attack she'd had in a long time. But the thought of those people taking Dinah away had made all of Josie's rational thoughts go right out of her frazzled mind. She'd done what she had to do.

She'd removed Dinah from the situation.

Only once she had Dinah, they didn't have time to grab anything much to travel with. So she'd come here, where she'd wait until dark, and then they'd sneak out. She'd only had time to grab some snack food and a change of clothes for Dinah.

Josie sank down against the wall. "Dinah, I've made a big mistake."

Dinah turned and slanted her head. Then she ran into Josie's arms. "Walk?"

"No more walk," Josie said. "We have to wait until dark. We have to stay here and then we walk—somewhere."

"Go," Dinah said, heading toward the closed door. "Go home."

Josie's eyes filled with tears. "I don't know where home is anymore."

She looked around her and let the tears flow. Dinah saw her crying and toddled back to her.

Her big eyes wide, the little girl's chubby fingers wiped Josie's face. "Boo-boo."

"A big boo-boo," Josie said, the tears falling freely now. Taking Dinah into her arms, she said, "You know I love you. So much."

"So muk," Dinah echoed, her fingers

warm against Josie's face. Then Dinah kissed her with a big smack. "No boo-boo."

Josie wrapped her arms around her daughter, every fiber of her mother's heart wanting to protect this child from all the ugliness of the world out there. "Safe, Dinah," she whispered. "I have to keep you safe."

And the only way to do that was to take Dinah back home, where she had people to protect her.

Wiping her eyes, Josie heaved a breath and stood. Then she heard footsteps coming up the stairs.

Someone had figured out where they were.

Josie held Dinah and realized there was no way out anyway.

Tobias opened the door to the room that used to be Josie's bedroom, the same room where she'd brought her baby once before.

"I had a feeling," he said, a tired smile moving over his face. "Everyone scattered, searching for you two, but I just knew you'd come here first."

Josie tried to speak. Dinah looked at her and then at Tobias. "JoJo cry."

Tobias rushed across the room and held them both close, his own eyes wet with tears. "JoJo is safe now, Dinah. And so are you."

Two days later, Josie and Tobias sat with the Beningtons at their home in Kentucky. Josie remembered the large paneled den with the big fireplace. Today the room was cool with air-conditioning, and a big square swimming pool shimmered blue just beyond the floor-to-ceiling windows and doors covering one wall.

A hospital bed had been placed in the corner, near a full bathroom. And in that bed lay Drew Benington.

She looked back from the beautiful gardens and stared at Drew. "You've seen her," she said, referring to Dinah. "We have to go back home tomorrow."

Drew nodded, barely able to speak, his eyes on the little girl sitting on a plush floral rug, playing with a teddy bear her grandparents had given her.

"She is so beautiful, Josie."

Tobias stared at his friend and then gave Josie a reassuring look. "She is in good hands, Drew. She is well loved."

Drew nodded, his once thick blond hair gone, his once healthy physique now shriveled. "I need you both to forgive me. I am so sorry. So very sorry. I'm not asking because I'm dying. I'm telling you this for Dinah's sake. Take care of her, and... I want you both to be happy."

Josie swallowed all the pain and hatred she'd felt for this man, her emotions pouring over her with a soothing release. She had to forgive. That was the Amish way. She and Tobias had talked about this on the long ride here in Nathan's SUV. He'd insisted on driving them to Kentucky, because his job was to protect his clients.

They had decided they could tolerate this visit only by forgiving Drew. He had confessed, he had asked for forgiveness and he was dying. What more could he suffer?

Facing the man who had assaulted her had been the most difficult thing Josie had ever done, but with Tobias by her side, she was at peace. At last.

They sat for a while longer, and then, after leaving Drew sleeping, they moved to the front hallway with his parents.

"We can never thank you enough," Pamela said. "We understand how difficult this has been, but once he saw her picture, he wanted to see her."

Josie refrained from what she wanted to say. "Dinah won't remember much about this, but this was the only way I could find peace, the same peace Drew is seeking. I forgive your son for what he did. I love my child, and my brother and Raesha love her dearly, too."

Tobias held Dinah and stood with Josie. "I love this one, too," he said, smiling at Dinah. "And I pray you will respect the terms Alisha came up with for us."

"We will abide by the terms," Theodore said. "We promised Drew we would."

They would get to visit Dinah several times a year, but Dinah would never know they were her paternal grandparents.

They'd offered money to help, which Josiah and Raesha had turned down.

"If you ever need anything," Theodore said again.

"*Denke*," Josie replied, "but you have given us the only thing we need. Dinah is ours and that now includes both of you. We are thankful that we were able to work things out."

Pamela kissed Dinah and then hugged Josie. "We will never forget what you've given to us, either."

They hurried to the sleek SUV and got Dinah tucked into the car seat between them in the back. As the vehicle pulled out of the circular driveway of the big brick house, Josie took one last look before she turned and smiled at Tobias.

"It's over," he said, his eyes full of love and hope. "Now we can start our new life together."

Drew died a week later.

Tobias came and told them on Sunday.

"Walk with me," he said to Josie after they'd all sat silent with their prayers.

She didn't hesitate. He guided her toward the house. Already it had changed. He'd built two rocking chairs and placed them on the front porch. Then he'd added a swing in her favorite corner spot with the view. Jewel had helped him pick out colorful potted plants for the porch.

He took Josie to the swing. "Will you sit with me?"

She laughed. "*Ja*, of course."

Tobias took her hand. "Josie, I love you and I want to marry you. Before you answer, I need to know one thing."

Her heart couldn't take much more. Had she done something wrong again? "What?"

"Will you be able to live here with me? Because if you cannot, I will sell this place and find us another house. Abram says there is a big farm for sale near his place."

Josie put a finger to his lips, her heart full of love.

"Tobias, I spent about four hours in this house last week with Dinah. She prattled and played while I worried. But I prayed, too. I prayed so hard, and I thought of you and me and how long it's taken us to find each other again." Heaving a deep breath, she said, "I could see it all so clearly sitting in the room I used to sleep in. The soul of a house is only as good as the people who live there. I lived in this house and grew up in this house, but I lost my soul when my parents died."

"So you don't want to be here?"

She looked at the man she loved and held back tears. "I didn't want to be here back then, but wherever you are, that is my home. I will marry you and I will make this our home. It will be full of love and children, and we have Dinah right across the way. It is enough. More than enough. This will be a fine home, and... I think my *mamm* will know I am safe here now. With you."

"Will I be enough?" he asked, his arms pulling her close.

"Always," she whispered, kissing his face with feathery little smacks. "More than enough. I love you. I'll always love you."

Tobias kissed her, and then he guided her to the front door. After opening it, he lifted her in his arms and took her inside.

"*Wilkum* home, Josie."

Josie smiled and kissed him again. Then she looked around and saw clusters of sunflowers in various vases all over the big living room. "How?"

Tobias laughed. "Jewel knows a lot of people who know how to get sunflowers shipped out early."

Josie touched her hand to his jaw. "I love Jewel. And I love you."

Tobias kissed her, and then together they lit the lamps and toured their new home while the setting sun shot rays of creamy-golden light through the windows, the kind of light that banished the darkness forever and washed their newfound love in the sweet grace of God.

* * * * *

Dear Reader,

This was a very emotional book to write. Josie had a tough life all of her life, so she made some bad choices. But she had a heart grounded in love and hope. Coming back to Campton Creek was the hardest thing she'd ever done, but with the love and support of her neighbors who had become her family, she found a place where she felt safe.

Tobias only wanted to start fresh and, hopefully, find the woman who'd left him and find out why she'd done so. He took a leap of faith and came to Campton Creek to start a new life and find Josie again. A horrible act forced them apart, but the love of family and the grace of God brought them back together and taught them the true meaning of forgiveness.

I hope this story brought you some hope and that it might have helped you in your own suffering. I fell in love with Campton Creek and all of the characters who showed up there. I hope you did, too. I'm working on a suspense set there now. But this book will stay in my heart for a long time to come.

Until next time,
May the angels watch over you. Always,

Lenora Worth